LUIS OF GUADALAJARA

By
JAMES MITCHELL CLARKE

Illustrated by
DAVID HENDRICKSON

PREPARED UNDER THE DIRECTION OF THE
CALIFORNIA STATE CURRICULUM COMMISSION

CALIFORNIA STATE SERIES

Published by
CALIFORNIA STATE DEPARTMENT OF EDUCATION
SACRAMENTO 1956

AUDIO-VISUAL AIDS

A series of five films relating to the subject matter of this book and of the two companion volumes, *The Adventures of Nicolás,* and *The People of Mexico,* has been produced by and is available from Paul Hoefler Productions, 7934 Santa Monica Boulevard, Los Angeles 46, California, with the collaboration of the California State Curriculum Commission and the Bureau of Audio-Visual Education of the California State Department of Education. The titles of the films are as follows: Guadalajara Home, Mexican Village Life, Mexican Village Family, Mexico at Work, Mexico's Heritage.

In addition to these films Paul Hoefler Productions is also producing a series of film strips and study prints dealing with the content of each of the three books.

printed in
CALIFORNIA STATE PRINTING OFFICE
SACRAMENTO 1ST PRINT, 125M 1956

For Elena
and Margarita

CONTENTS

		Page
Letter of Introduction		1

CHAPTER

1. My Friend and My City	7
2. My Father's Secret	21
3. Children of the Sun	33
4. Don Sebastián and the Sick Baby	45
5. Luis Goes to the "Cats," and Afterward Gets His Face Dirty	52
6. The Adventure at Doña Josefa's	67
7. My Father Decides	80
8. Things That "Sell Themselves Crying"	91
9. I Behave Very Badly	104
10. We Go to the "Center"	113
11. Raquel Asks for an Egg	127
12. A Star of *Chiles*	144

		Page
13.	How Pidal Took in Luis	158
14.	Luis and the Flying Bulls	166
15.	The Hunt Through the Market	189
16.	The Big Lie	206
17.	"Go, Little Fly!"	220
18.	High Above the City	226
19.	We Hunt for Luis	240
20.	We Learn More About Pidal, and I Visit the Toy-makers	259
21.	Dark, Lonesome Road	276
22.	Don Arturo and the Hummingbird	285
23.	Our Lady of Zapopan—and Pidal	304
24.	The Golden Egg	316
25.	I Build a New Home	331
	Postscript	346
	Spanish and Indian Words Used in This Book	347

Guadalajara, Jalisco, Republic of Mexico
365 Calle de los Pastores

Dear Friends in California:

I want to thank you and your families once again for inviting me to visit in your homes. It was a wonderful experience—seeing California from end to end, with your help.

As you already know, each of you is invited to come and stay in my house in Guadalajara. But it is just as far from San Francisco to Guadalajara as from San Francisco to Kansas City, Missouri.

1

When I looked up these distances on a map, I was interested. Kansas City is near the middle of your country; Guadalajara is near the middle of mine. Anyhow, I am afraid that some of you may not get down to visit me.

This makes me sad, for I want so much for you to know my city. We *Tapatíos* (that is what the people of Guadalajara are called—*Tapatíos*) love Guadalajara the way a child loves its beautiful mother.

But how can one tell about his mother in a way that makes others understand her and love her? This is what I want to do for you, just in case you should not be able to come and meet my city for yourselves.

When I spoke of this to my father, he began to smile as he does when he is remembering exciting, pleasant things.

"Why don't you tell them the story of Luis?" my father said. "All of us learned to know Guadalajara better through him. What a boy is that Luis!"

My father is right; he usually is. I did not really know Guadalajara before we came to know Luis. He was born to have adventures as the

sparks fly up the chimney. Anyone who becomes Luis's friend is sure to find life full of surprises, not all of them pleasant, to be sure, but all of them interesting and many of them exciting.

I know many stories about Luis, and there will be others as he grows older. Luis is the kind of person who lives stories. The one my father wants me to tell you happened a few years ago—before I came to visit in California. At that time, I was ten and Luis had thirteen years, as we say in Spanish. But I remember everything as if it had happened yesterday, and I understand better what happened because everyone who was mixed up in these adventures talked about them for months afterward. I know what everyone did and said as well as if I had seen and heard it all.

Your friend who misses you,

MARTÍN

P. S. I asked Mr. Johnson, who was mixed up in the most exciting times we had with Luis, to make all the English just right in my story. He would not touch it. He said that I sometimes used English in a Spanish way. But he thinks that you will understand everything best if it comes straight from my heart.

I also asked Mr. Johnson whether I should tell about Guadalajara the way it is now, or the way it was when Luis had his adventures.

"Are you and Luis any different, now?" he asked me.

"Of course we are," I said.

"Would you have had the same adventures if you had been the same in those days as you are now?"

I shook my head.

"Well then," said Mr. Johnson, "you'd better write about the city as it was, because the adventures would not happen quite the same in the Guadalajara we live in now. A city is like a person. A city changes from year to year, just as people

change. A city is a living thing. A book never changes because it is only words on paper. No book can ever be quite up to date. But this does not matter to us. Guadalajara is an old city and changes slowly—the way grownups slowly change. Once you have come to know and love Guadalajara, you understand and love it for always."

CHAPTER 1

My Friend and My City

I was at home, in the patio, making a clay model of our house. I had been very sick. The doctor said that if I got into a ball game or a wrestling match, or something like that, it would be very bad. He said I had to stay in the house until I was all well. But he also said that I had to stay outdoors as much as I could.

Not many of you could be inside the house and be outdoors at the same time. But in Mexico this is very easy. Most houses in the city—and the bigger houses in the towns, also—are built around a large patio. Our house has two patios.

The one where I was working is in the middle of the house. Its floor is made of rose-colored tiles with blue designs. Anselmo was swishing them with a big mop rag tied to a stick. The tiles glistened. The bright leaves of the plants growing in the patio glistened too, because Anselmo had just watered them. Cleaning up and tending to the growing things and running errands are Anselmo's job. He comes from a village called Santa Cruz, where most of the people make toys out of clay. Anselmo helped me out sometimes with my model, but it was not like having another boy to work with.

I had a lonesome and tired feeling as I stood there, smoothing arches and trying to make all the columns the same size. The arches go all the way around our patio, and behind them is a wide porch that is always cool, even on the brightest days. It was hard to make these arches small, and in clay. I stopped often and stood there just thinking and wishing.

Anselmo went into the kitchen and through it into the back patio. He must have left the door open. I heard the ducks quack and the pigeons coo. Most of the old houses in Guadalajara have

8

these second patios back of the house. They were built so that every family could have its own farmyard, right inside the house. We call them *corrales*. In ours we have orange trees and avocados and other fruit; also ducks, chickens, and a pigeon loft. Of course we could buy fruit and fowls in the market, but my father likes to live in the old-fashioned way.

The sounds from the *corral* set me to thinking about Luis. I began to feel sorry for myself. Why was I not Luis? Why should he get to have all the fun?

Most people would smile at me for having these thoughts. Luis did not have a house for a home, nor a mother to love him and care for him. I will tell you by and by where Luis slept.

His father owned some burros and went about the country with them, buying and selling. Now that Luis had finished the sixth grade, he went with his father all the time, instead of just in vacations as he had before.

Why should I, Martín Mendosa, wish I were Luis? Because he made everything he did seem like fun. And because he had gone among the high, green mountains of Michoacán, the state that lies next to Jalisco on the south. Who would not be happy to go to Michoacán, where the lakes are mirrors held up high so that the sky can see her beautiful face! I would go there any time I could. And at the time I am telling of, I had been kept in the house a whole month, remember.

I was still wishing that I were Luis when the knocker hammered on the door of our house. The door is big enough for a carriage to drive through, and the knocker is an iron lion. When anyone knocks, the sound goes through the house like thunder—boom, boom, boom!

Anselmo went to open the smaller door that is cut into the big one. I heard him give a small, pleased shout. The next minute, Luis himself came hurrying into the patio.

"Martín!" he called. "How good that you are up out of your bed and working here in the open air! I am so glad!"

Then he saw my mother, who had just come out into the porch behind the arches, carrying a bit of sewing.

"Excuse me!" said Luis, taking off his big hat with the high peak, "I did not see you. I hope you are very well, Señora, and also your husband, Don Agustín, and Doña Lucía, your beautiful daughter!"

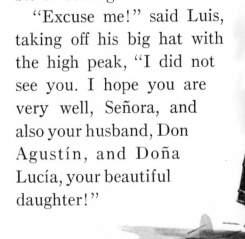

He was apologizing for not having spoken to my mother before he spoke to me. But my mother did not even think of that. She has a sweet smile that comes slowly to her face and stays there a long time. She was smiling all the way as she walked out into the patio and put her arms around Luis.

"How wonderful that you have come back!" she said, patting him on the head. "You were away a long time."

Luis and I hugged each other. Friends in Mexico do this when they meet. But I think we would have hugged each other if we had been Americans—we were that glad to see each other.

"I am very mad with you," I said, holding Luis by the shoulders and looking up into his face. "Why did you stay away from us so long?"

You must know that Luis is not beautiful. He has a snub nose; his mouth is too big, and his eyes are a little too small. But you have seldom seen eyes like those. As my mother says, "Other people's eyes dance, but only Luis's eyes dance the *jarabe*."

The *jarabe tapatío* is the quick dance where the heels go like a machine gun with rhythm. Luis's big mouth goes with his eyes. When he smiles, it takes a very sad man—or a very bad one, like Señor Pidal—to keep from smiling also. Now he smiled down at me, for, as I told you, he was thirteen and I was only ten.

"When you hear what happened to us," he said, "you will wonder how we ever got home at all. The mud was so deep the burros became submarines and breathed through their ears!"

Isabela, our cook, was standing in the doorway of our kitchen. Isabela is something you seldom see, a fat Indian—fat and jolly, with a heart bigger than her stomach, which is a remarkable sight itself. Also, in the words of my father—who sometimes shocks my mother—she could cook for the blessed angels in heaven.

Luis ran to her and Isabela hugged him. She loves him almost as much as I.

Mother laughed and called to Isabela to bring us cakes and something cold to drink. We got pineapple juice, made that very hour by squeezing pieces of the yellow fruit in a cloth. We three, Luis and my mother and I, sat at a small table with a marble top, in the cool, covered porch beside the patio.

Luis did not look like a boy you would expect to find at the table with my mother. True, he had put on fresh overalls and shirt. But the old woman who kept house for Luis and his father had not gotten all the dirt out of his clothes when she washed. It was the same with his hands. I mean he had not quite gotten the dirt of hard travel out of them. I could see from his damp hair and shining face that he had just bathed; but it is hard to get the hands clean when one bathes by splashing cold water on himself from a bucket. Where Luis lives there is no tub, nor any shower. To get hot water, they must heat it over a charcoal fire.

But it was natural for Luis to be at the table with my mother. Our neighborhood is something special. It is one of the *barrios* into which the city was divided when still a young town.

Each one has its own market and its own church and its own garden. Each has a name. We understand the people in our own *barrio* a little better than the people of anywhere else. To be born and grow up in one of the old *barrios* is rather like belonging to a large family.

Besides, my mother liked to have Luis around because he cheered me up. He always remembered to come to visit me when he was in the city. The oftener he came, the more glad we all were to see him.

On the trip to Michoacán, Luis and his father had taken oranges and brought back lacquered plates and bowls. The summer rains fell like waterfalls, and their burros traveled so slowly that they sometimes could not reach a village before night fell. Once they slept in a roofless, ruined church during a driving storm. They nearly lost a burro where a stretch of road had slid down a steep mountainside.

Luis did not skip the hard work or the dangerous parts. But he made it all seem exciting, and a lot of it was comical, the way he told it— like the time he tried to pull the burro out of a deep mudhole by tugging on the bridle.

"There was I," he said, throwing himself back in his chair with his hands raised and his legs stretched out to show how he had fallen down. "There was I, sitting in a mud puddle. And there was the burro, looking me right in the face. He rolled his eyes, and he gave me a crooked grin. 'Brother,' he said, 'I don't know which one of us is the biggest jackass to get into this, but neither of us has got any business here!'"

Of course Luis didn't believe that the burro talked to him, but he insisted that he really had. About important things Luis tells the truth, but when he tells a story he tries to make you believe any crazy thing.

My mother left us after the story, and I took Luis over to show him my house. I had made it on an old table, set in one of the archways. I could work in the patio during the cool times and move around onto the porch when it got hot and bright. It was afternoon now. The light touched the model in just the right way to make it look its best.

Luis made me feel very good when he looked at my model, for he praised all the things I was proud of—the coat of arms beside the door, the gratings for the windows I had made out of wire, the smooth curves of the arches around the patio, the fountain in the center.

"And look!" he said. "Here is even a stove that cooks with gas, and a real bathroom all sanitary with plumbing of the American kind, just like yours. And here is Don Agustín in his study and your mother in her sewing room. You will be a great architect one of these days, Martín."

I was ashamed to show how pleased I was at his praise, so I said, "My mother found the stove and things for the bathroom in a store downtown. She bought the little figures of the people in the market. But she could not find Isabela."

Luis laughed. "Nobody makes people so fat as Isabela. What is this, Martín?"

He was pointing to some walls that I had made beside my house. I told him that I had started to make the house of our neighbor Don Porfirio. In fact, I had the plan of making the whole block and getting it done to surprise Luis when he came home.

"But that was before I found out how long it took to make the house only," I said. "It would be much too much work to make the block."

"You got discouraged because you were working alone," Luis said, putting his arm around me. "Together we could build the block easily. We could build the whole city of Guadalajara if we wanted to. Come on!"

He dipped up a big ball of clay from the jar beside the table and started building up the walls of Don Porfirio's house. It always makes me blink to see Luis go to work, because he does everything so fast. I knew that he would build two inches of wall to every one I built. But I also knew that I would have to straighten and smooth the walls after he got through.

CHAPTER 2

My Father's Secret

I did not know my father had come home until I heard his voice behind me, speaking very low. He was saying, "Luis is a dreamer. But how can we build Mexico without men who dream—and other men, like our Martín, who make the dreams come true?"

"And which are you?" asked my mother's clear, sweet voice.

"You know very well," said my father. "I am no dreamer. That is my weakness. Because I could build but could not dream, I did not become an architect, though I studied to be one."

"There is many a fine dream that would not have come true in Guadalajara except for you," said my mother. "We would not have an airline to the Pacific Coast if you had not taken hold and made the planes fly on time and with safety. Where would the factory that makes cooking oil be, except for you? A plan on paper, gathering dust in somebody's office—that is where the factory would be. And what about the new school for boys, and the new room for the little babies in the hospital, and——"

My father stopped her with his laugh. "If I seemed as wonderful to others as I seem to my wife," my father said, "they would be wanting me to run for president of Mexico, instead of mayor * of Guadalajara."

* In Guadalajara we call the head of our city government Municipal President. But it is better to use the words you use in your country, when they have the same meaning as our words, so I use the word "mayor." It gives the right idea.

I could not keep on pretending that I did not hear. I turned straight around and stared at my father. It was very still for a second—so still that I could hear the water gurgling out of the stone fishes' mouths in the fountain behind me. I threw myself on my father, asking questions so fast he could not possibly answer them.

"Gently!" my father said. "It is nothing to be so excited about, Son. I have not even decided that I want to be mayor. It is not at all sure that the people would want me."

"Of course they would want you!" said Luis. He also had turned to my father, and his small black eyes had a light of excitement as bright as the sunshine sparkling on the big silver pin at my mother's throat. "You would be the best mayor Guadalajara ever had!"

My father has a lean, dark, serious face. His eyes look very straight at you, and you can tell by his mouth that he will stick to what he says he will do. Yet when he smiles as he was smiling at Luis now, it makes you feel good—even though he is partly making fun of you. He said, "Thank you, Luis. It is good to know that I have my friends behind me."

"Just tell me what I can do to help!" said Luis, standing very straight. "I will do anything, Don Agustín!"

My father's smile grew a little sad, I thought. He spoke more to himself than to Luis. "The first thing is to make Arturo Amador understand that he must help."

"What is wrong with Don Arturo Amador?" Luis asked fiercely. "Doesn't he know that you would be the best mayor ever?"

My father pulled me around to his side and put his other arm around Luis. "Never mind," he said. "Let us not speak of this any more. Not to anyone, you understand!"

We both said, *"Sí, señor!* (Yes, sir!)"

"I depend on you to keep this secret," my father said, "until the right time. Just now, let us interest our- selves in Luis's plan to make Guadalajara in clay. If I become mayor, my son should know more about our city than other boys know.

24

If I do not become mayor—then we will have Guadalajara anyway. A clay city is better than none."

"But how could we make the whole city?" I wanted to know. "Just making our house took me a long, long time."

My father turned us around and took us into the *sala* (parlor). In many homes in Guadalajara, the *sala* is a stuffy place, used only at times so important that the people feel stiff. Our *sala* is a pleasant room; my father and mother often have interesting people there to talk. When I was little, I used to get up out of bed and stand on the porch where I could look into the *sala* without being seen. I liked to see the women in their pretty dresses and hear their gay voices as they talked and laughed with the men in their white, starched shirts.

The shutters were open toward the afternoon sun. It was so bright that the iron bars at the windows seemed thin and delicate as vines with wrought-iron leaves. The light made the pictures glow on the wall.

We have four paintings in the *sala*. Two of them, museums would be glad to have. They

25

were painted by my great-great-grandfather, the
one who planned and built our house. One of
these pictures shows the *sala* itself. A woman is
standing with one hand on the small, carved
table of rosy wood where I had put my own
hand when we came into the room.

"Look closely," my father said. "Notice the
things the artist has shown all of, then the things
he has shown part of, and then the things he has
left to your imagination."

It was easy enough to see what he meant. Above the table, everything about the woman— eyes, lips, even the jewel at her throat—was clear as life; but below, there was only enough to give you the notion of long skirts reaching to the floor and little silk slippers peeping out from beneath them. There was just enough of the window and the other furniture to let you know what was in the room.

My father also had us look carefully at the picture of Chapala, the big lake near Guadalajara. The boats and fishermen near the shore were very clear, but the mountains across the lake were just blue shapes.

"This is how you will make Guadalajara," my father said. "You will do it the same way an artist gets a whole room, or even a lake, onto two feet of canvas."

For a minute we stood looking at him very much puzzled and worried because we did not understand. Then the light struck us at the same moment.

"I get it!" said Luis, striking his fist into his palm. "We just make the important things and show where the others are."

"And when we make a house or building," I said, "we build only the parts that make it look like itself."

My father put one hand on my shoulder and his other hand on Luis's shoulder. "Between the two of you," he said, "you understand very well."

We went back into the patio and planned how we would do it. My father promised to get some smooth planks to go on sawhorses to make a big, rough table. On the planks we could draw the streets with chalk, as far out as San Pedro Tlaquepaque, where the pottery is made, and the other towns nearby. The farther out we went toward the edge of the city, the smaller we would

28

make the blocks. The biggest block would be our own—the block we lived in.

It was hard to decide what other buildings we would make, because we got to arguing. We could not even agree on the important places in our own *barrio*. Luis wanted to make the market and the stable where his father kept his burros when he was in the city. I wanted to make our neighborhood church and the theater.

"You have not even remembered the schools," my father said. "Martín, your ancestor—the man who built this house—wrote some wise words in his diary: 'An artist does not know his own wife's face until he starts to paint her picture.' This is the way it has turned out with you boys—you have lived in Guadalajara all your lives, but you do not even know your own *barrio* well enough to make its picture in clay."

We asked him what we should do.

"Luis will have to be eyes for both of you—and ears, too. The important places are the ones people use most in their daily lives and the ones they have most often in their thoughts. Therefore Luis must find out how people live. And while he is about it he should learn all about the people themselves, so that you can put people in the streets. Otherwise your city will be as dead as the deserted city of the Mayas at Chichén Itzá.

I will buy you all the little figures you need, as soon as you have decided on the ones you want."

With that my father left us, and we fell to work on the house next door to ours. It is a nice house, though not so nice as ours or so large as ours. I can make you see it by drawing you a picture better than I can make you see it in words.

"Four of the houses in your block are about like this one," said Luis, as he rolled a "snake" of clay between his hands. "Only yours and Doña Josefa's house are different."

"Doña Josefa's place is big enough for three houses," I said. "You could call it a palace."

"Have you been there?" Luis wanted to know.

"Two or three times. The first time I was too little to remember much. The other times I went after dark. We will have to ask my mother what it is like."

"No," Luis said, putting his clay snake on a half-finished wall and smoothing it with his thumb. "It is better to put into our model only things we see with our own eyes and understand for ourselves. In that way, it will be our own city that we make."

"But how will you get in?" I asked. "Doña Josefa is away—in New York or France or some far place. Those sugar-cane farms and sugar mills she owns make her so rich that she has to go away from home to spend her money. The servants never let anyone into her house. I used to imagine that strange, mysterious things went on in there. It is such a secret, big house. But my father says no, there are no mysteries."

We worked busily for a while without talking.

"The only near relation Doña Josefa has in Guadalajara is Don Arturo Amador," I said, after a time. "He is her nephew. But we cannot get permission from him to go into Doña Josefa's house. He is also a relation of ours in some far-off way, but he and my father do not ask favors of one another."

With the back of his hand, Luis pushed a fan of his straight, black hair away from his eyes; the palm of his hand was all sticky with clay. His bright, black eyes were full of questions.

"Why are your father and Don Arturo not friends?"

"I have heard my father and mother talk of Don Arturo and it seems to be like this. My father does not think well of Don Arturo's business. He does not think that bringing bullfighters and prize fighters to Guadalajara are good ways to make money. Don Arturo thinks my father is too serious."

Luis stood still for a time and thought about this. Then he shrugged his shoulders and picked up a lump of clay with a quick grasp. "Anyhow," he said, "I will get into Doña Josefa's house. I am going there tomorrow."

32

CHAPTER 3

Children of the Sun

When Luis opened his eyes next morning, all he could see was a golden thread. It ran straight down the darkness of the room, for the thread was sunlight coming through the narrow crack between the shutters drawn tight across the window. Luis listened. His father's strong snore came steadily and peacefully. But the old, wheezy snore of his godmother he could not hear. She must already be up and gone to the market.

33

Luis's bed was made of canvas stretched between poles. It could be folded up against the
wall, out of the way. With all three beds in the
room, it was so crowded one could hardly move.
It was rather dark most of the day, even with
the shutters open. Neither Luis nor his father
stayed in the room any more than he had to.

Luis slipped quietly out of bed, found his
clothes where they hung against the wall, and
began to dress quickly. He was thinking about
Doña Josefa's house. One did not have to go out
of a house like that. Each person had a room to
himself and other rooms he could go to. Beautiful
rooms they must be, yet Doña Josefa was always
going away. "Why did she leave her fine house?"
Luis wondered, as he buttoned his shirt.

It was surprising, he thought, how many questions came to mind when a person really tried
to find out how his neighbors lived. Life was full
of new, interesting things, full of puzzles and
small mysteries. He slipped his sweater over his
head. Rain during the night had left a little chill
in the air. His fingers caught in a hole in the
sleeve of his sweater as he shoved his arm
through. He tore the hole bigger before he

realized what he was doing. A new idea had come to Luis, so interesting that it pushed everything else out of his mind.

"I live in this neighborhood, too," he thought. "I am not so important as Don Agustín and Martín. Nobody would print it in the papers if I went away. Yet there are a good many who would miss my father and me if anything happened to us. We are part of the life here. Since this is so, Martín and I must put something of my life into our model. The houses of the rich are just one part of our *barrio*—the prettiest part. We must build the place I live in, also; we must build this *vecindad* (tenement house)."

It seemed to Luis that the room where he and his father lived would be enough to show the life inside. All the rooms were very much alike, though in some of them the women had put pretty curtains and little altars with statues of saints and vases for flowers. In the bigger rooms so many people lived that they were even more crowded than in Luis's home.

As Luis slipped quietly through the door, it came to him that the inside is not the important thing about a *vecindad*. There was his old friend the sun, pouring warm light into the courtyard. Already the dampness from last night's rain was beginning to dry. Luis stretched his arms and began to smile. Outside, where the sun could reach it, the *vecindad* was not a bad place. And outside was where the people really lived.

In this moment of early morning, Luis had come upon an important truth about Mexicans. We are children of the sun, which never leaves Mexico as it leaves the north in winter. The most important part of any house or *vecindad* is the patio. We like to buy and sell in the open. We like to go about the streets and roads, stopping to talk with one another. Our happiest times are *fiestas,* when we gather in the open air. We like to eat out of doors.

In front of Luis's door, on the edge of the porch, stood a brick stove. A small fire of charcoal was burning under a clay pot. Luis's godmother had left water for coffee to heat while she went to market. A big clay pitcher stood beside the stove. Luis poured water into the half of a big, round gourd, the kind that grows on trees and is called a calabash. He washed his face,

then combed his hair in front of a cracked mirror that hung to a pillar. He leaned against the pillar, looking about the courtyard to make sure that he remembered everything well enough to build the *vecindad* into our model.

On each side of the courtyard were five doors, leading into five rooms, in which five families lived. Running in front of these doors was a porch with high arches and thin pillars made of stone, which showed here and there through holes in the plaster. The walls were of stone, also covered with chipped plaster.

In front of each door was a stove like Luis's. From each stove came the smoke of a charcoal fire, a very thin smoke that lost itself in the sunshine. Around almost every stove was a little group of people—at the least, a couple of women fanning the fire and patting out *tortillas;* at the most, a half-dozen children with their father and mother. The whole courtyard was filled with a pleasant sound of people chatting and laughing together. Sometimes voices would rise as neighbors called to one another. Some children darted into the middle of the courtyard, chased each other out beyond the laundry tubs, and came back panting and laughing to their breakfast.

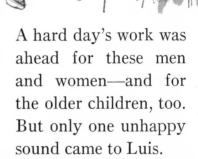

A hard day's work was ahead for these men and women—and for the older children, too. But only one unhappy sound came to Luis.

Inside the room next to his, a woman was scolding in a high, angry voice. A child wailed.

That would be little Conchita, Luis thought. Probably she had wakened her mother, Doña Magdalena—who would have a better temper if she stayed home nights.

Luis picked up the water pitcher and went down to the laundry tubs, which stood in a row beside a small, plain building in the middle of the courtyard. Half of this building was the bath; the rest, the toilet for all the families. This was the worst of living in a *vecindad*.

The laundry tubs were made of stone, with a flat part having grooves for scrubbing and a square basin for washing. Luis filled his water pitcher at the tap. The plumber's wife and the wife of the herb-seller were getting water from the next basin.

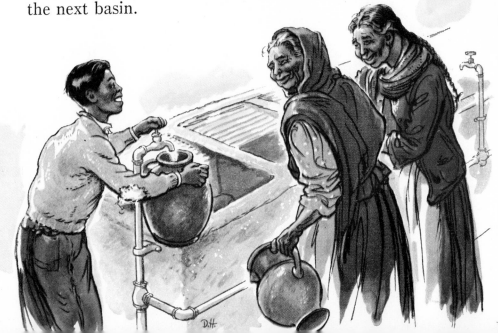

They were friendly women. Their brown skins were wrinkled, but their lively eyes showed that they were not so old as they looked at first sight.

They said good morning to Luis and asked if his father was in good health. By the look on their faces, Luis could see that they were asking in their minds a question that the neighbors often asked of Luis, "When is Don Sebastián going to get a new mother for you?"

They did not dare any more to ask Luis's father this question to his face. He felt that it was his own private affair that he did not choose to marry again, and it annoyed him to have people tell him what to do. No one cared to have Don Sebastián really angry with him.

The plumber's wife reached out and pulled at a thread sticking from the hole in the sleeve of Luis's sweater. "It's too bad there is no one to take care of your clothes, Luis," she said.

Before Luis could think what to say, a dried-up little man, very bent and feeble, came shuffling up with his bucket. He sold *chiles* (peppers) in the *barrio* market. He should have been there by the time the sun was up. The plumber's wife asked him if he was sick.

He answered that it was his daughters' day off. This explained everything to the others. His daughter worked as a maid to a family in our own block. On her days off, she took her father's place in the market.

"Pobrecita! (Poor little thing!)" said the herb-seller's wife. "Sometimes I think my life is hard. My husband and I travel many hard miles on foot when we go to the mountains to gather plants that cure the sick. But think of this poor child! Never a moment to be free and do a little something for herself."

"A woman with children works as hard as she does," said the plumber's wife. "But she has her children to give her pleasure."

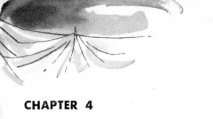

CHAPTER 4

Don Sebastián and the Sick Baby

Luis left the neighbor women still chattering. He passed his left arm behind his head so that he could steady with his hand the pitcher riding on his right shoulder. Beside the stove, his father stood waiting for the water. Luis filled the half-gourd for him before he set the pitcher down.

Don Sebastián washed his face, combed his hair, and stood looking out across the courtyard. He stood very still, but without trying to be still. His strong hand, with the fingers a little curled, hung beside him as if it had been carved from stone. He had a rocklike look. As men go, he was small, but his chest was very deep. His whole body was a solid mass of muscle. He had the same snub nose as Luis, but his face seldom changed and his eyes were so light they were almost gray. The blood ran close to his skin and gave him that ruddy look so many of our Guadalajara people have. He and Luis did not look alike at all.

45

"Where is *la vieja* (the old woman)?" Don Sebastián asked. "Gone to the market?"

Luis said that she had been gone quite a while and ought to be back soon. Don Sebastián did not answer or move. Luis, being talkative, often felt as if he were chattering to a rock when he tried to talk to his father. Yet Luis felt comfortable and safe when he was with Don Sebastián, even though he might be silent for hours. They understood each other. Now they both watched a big man with a sad face who was coming toward them with dragging feet. Though his face and hands were clean, a small bad smell came ahead of him. This was Don Bartolo, the garbage man, on his way to work. He could not afford enough clothes so that the dirty ones could be washed each day.

When Don Bartolo came near, he made a motion that meant he wanted Don Sebastián to come to him. Don Sebastián stepped forward like a rock leaving its place on a steep hillside, swiftly, but smoothly.

Don Bartolo began to speak softly. He kept his head down and looked unhappy, as if he were doing something he did not like to do. The people in the courtyard were making less noise than usual. In the half-stillness Luis heard the small, unhappy cry of a sick child. Don Bartolo threw out his hand toward the sound, then turned back to Don Sebastián and spoke more quickly. Beyond the two men, Luis saw his old godmother coming into the courtyard. She carried a basket covered with the end of her *rebozo* (shawl).

Suddenly Don Sebastián lifted his hand as if to hit Don Bartolo. "Shut up!" he said in a loud, fierce voice.

The old godmother stopped her shuffling steps and stared at the men with her mouth open. Don Sebastián's lifted hand went behind him, as if for a weapon. But he only reached for his bill-fold. He took from it some paper money, which he pushed into Don Bartolo's hand.

He turned away from the man's thanks and walked with swift, angry steps back to Luis. He put his back against the pillar beside the stove and glared out across the courtyard. The old god-mother set her basket down and took from it *masa,* the sticky dough made by grinding corn softened in water with a pinch of lime. She began to pat out *tortillas,* and as she patted, she sniffed. The old woman did this when she disliked something Luis or his father had done. It always made her angriest of all when Don Sebastián lent money to friends and neighbors.

Luis knew that Don Bartolo must be in deep trouble. He had five small children, but his wife was clever at stretching money and they managed to get along on his small wage. It was unusual for him to borrow money. Luis had more than once seen his father act as if he were angry with people who told him their troubles. Don Sebastián could not stand to hear about suffering.

The old woman's sniffing made Luis cross. He moved over next to his father and put his own shoulder against Don Sebastián's arm. They stood without speaking until the old woman said crossly, *"Listo* (ready)." They took the *tortillas* she handed them, and turned their backs again. Don Sebastián tore off a bite of *tortilla* with his strong teeth.

"It is the little one," he said. "If Don Bartolo can keep on buying the medicines, he will get well. If not—there will be another *angelito* (little angel) in heaven."

Luis pushed a little harder against his father. "I would live on *tortillas* and coffee for a long time if it would keep that baby from dying. He likes me. He always laughs when I stop to talk with him; one time when his mother was bathing him out in the sunshine, he splashed water on me. That is the kind of small brother I would like."

His father stared gloomily over the courtyard. The shoemaker and the gardener and a man who unloaded freight from railroad cars passed by on their way to work. Don Sebastián only nodded in answer to their good mornings. At last he said, "Three years in this hole of a *vecindad!* I had hoped to get you out of here long ago, Luis."

"It is not so bad a place," Luis said. "I am not unhappy—except when we go on a trip after eggs. I hate bringing eggs on the burros. We have to be so careful and go so slowly that it drives me crazy."

"Don't be a fool, Luis! If I could get a few more burros and hire one or two men to help, we could make enough on eggs to get us out of this *vecindad*. You could go to a higher school and get somewhere in the world when you grow up. The way it is," Don Sebastián threw out his strong hands in a downhearted way, "there is never enough left when the expenses are paid to do us any good. The way things are going, it would take ten years to save enough to pay for the animals and the help I need to make money in the egg business. For the rich, and for those who have rich friends who will help them, there are many chances to make money. But a man who starts poor is like one who hunts with a bow and arrow—the chances to make money fly away before one has a shot at them."

It was not often that Don Sebastián spoke in such a discouraged way. He believed in himself. Usually he was full of hope and courage. Luis wanted to comfort him. He was about to say that their luck was bound to change soon, when the old woman broke in to tell them that more *tortillas* were ready and the coffee hot.

"I am not hungry," Don Sebastián said, and walked away from them. out of the *vecindad*.

CHAPTER 5

Luis Goes to the "Cats," and Afterward Gets His Face Dirty

When Luis came near Doña Josefa's house, he saw a man leaning against the wall beside the door. It was the middle of the morning, and the street was almost empty. When a Mexican street is empty, it is like a stage in an auditorium. The houses are all joined together, making a solid wall behind the sidewalk. Their pale colors—tan and gray and white, with here and there blue or pink—throw back the sun.

The man beside Doña Josefa's door was like someone standing against a curtain drawn across a stage, with the footlights full on him. He was a stranger to Luis. He had a yellowish face, and though he was wearing a business suit (our businessmen wear the same kind of suits as businessmen in the United States do), he looked rough. Luis pretended to be looking at the fat cupids carved on the big door of Doña Josefa's house, though he was really studying the man. All the while the man pretended to be looking at some pigeons across the street, when really he was studying Luis.

The man puzzled Luis, and worried him also. A neighbor who lived in the *barrio* might lounge against the wall all day without seeming suspicious. But a stranger might be intending to rob Doña Josefa's house. Or he might be on guard for some reason. If he was on guard, this was one more reason why Luis had to have a good excuse for asking to get into the house. And he had not yet thought of one that suited him.

A girl came hurrying across the street, halfway between Doña Josefa's house and my house. It was the *chile*-seller's daughter. Luis came up to her just as she was reaching for the knocker on the door of the home where she worked. In answer to Luis's questions, she said that she had come back to change her clothes. Her thin, unpretty face was all smiles. The plumber's wife and the wife of the herb-seller had scolded her father for half an hour without stopping. He finally gave up and came to take her place behind the stand where *chiles* were sold. The girl was going to the movies—for the first time in six months. Afterward, she would go to church.

Luis said he was sure that she would have a happy day. Then, with a little motion of his head toward the man beside Doña Josefa's door, he asked if she knew him. The girl shook her head. The man was a stranger, she said. Excusing herself politely, she raised the knocker.

"Wait," said Luis. "What is the name of Doña Josefa's cook?"

"Juanito," the girl said, and let the knocker fall with a bang, for she was in a hurry to get to the movies.

Luis walked back to Doña Josefa's. Without looking at the man, he knocked on the big door with the cupids. This had a smaller door cut into it. A maid stuck her head out, looking worried.

"Please," said Luis. "Is Juanito here?"

The maid answered that he was. "I've just got to see him," Luis went on. "You see, his old Aunt Amelia is very sick. I am Juanito's nephew. That is, my father and Juanito——"

A hoarse, whispering voice stopped Luis. "Go away, boy!" the voice said.

The man who had been leaning against the wall had moved up close beside him. Luis said, when he told me about it, that the man was looking at him the way a wolf looks out of a cage—staring with yellow eyes that did not blink. Like the wolf, he seemed to be hoping for a chance to hurt somebody.

"Go!" he said again in his strange, hoarse voice.

The maid slammed the door. *"Sí, señor!"* said Luis, and went off, walking fast. I am ashamed to say that I would have been afraid to go back to Doña Josefa's. But I am not Luis. The man on guard had made him very curious—and more determined than ever to get in.

He went to the "Cats," on the corner beside our *barrio* church. People go in and out of the church all day long. Also, all day long people come to walk or sit in the garden across the street. It is a large square, laid out with lawns and flower beds—a little park. The people of our *barrio* are very fond of it. Naturally, people want to talk when they come out of church. They stop for soft drinks and chatter at the Cats. These are stands on wheels, which are drawn up at the curb beside the church. Thirsty ones cross over from the garden.

There are three Cats, and the one nearest the corner is the oldest. The man who runs it has a way of listening that makes people feel free to talk. He knows practically everything that is going on in our *barrio*.

Luis asked him who the man was who stood outside the door of Doña Josefa's house. The man who runs the first Cat pulled at his black mustache. "All I know is that he came in a long black car with some other men. One of Doña Josefa's servants opened the door of the garage when the car came, and it drove right in. Very soon, this man came out, and he has been standing by the door ever since. I hear that you want to get into Doña Josefa's house so you and Martín Mendosa can build a copy of it in your model of Guadalajara. Is that right?"

"It is the truth," Luis said, grinning. "There is nothing you don't know! Tell me, then, how am I going to get in?"

"That is up to you," said the man. "But I did hear Doña Josefa's cook, Juanito, say that he was having trouble getting the charcoal-seller across the street to deliver some sacks of charcoal. The man says he won't deliver it unless Juanito helps him. Juanito says he won't help."

Luis's grin flashed once more. "Thanks, uncle," he said, and went away, running.

The charcoal-seller's place stood on a corner. It had one doorway on our street and one on the side street that also runs past Doña Josefa's. Luis ducked in the side-street door. The charcoal was heaped up in a corner, held in by a wooden wall reaching halfway to the ceiling and halfway across the small room. The charcoal-seller sat in a chair tilted back against this wall.

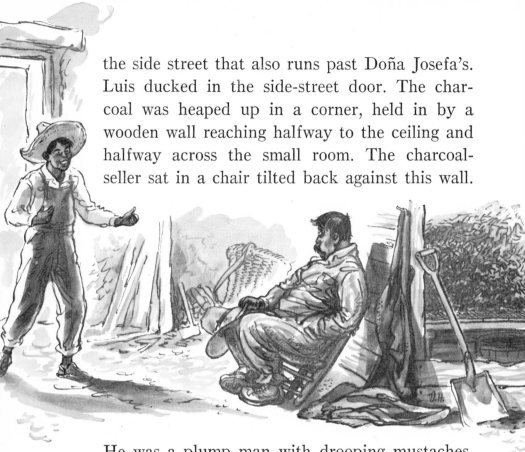

He was a plump man with drooping mustaches. His large, sad eyes looked out from a face so smudged with black that he looked like a very dirty child. The sad eyes rested gently on Luis, as if he were wondering what new trouble had come to him.

"Juanito sent me to help you bring the charcoal," Luis said brightly.

The man pulled himself slowly to his feet and sighed deeply. "Juanito should have come himself," he said. "But I am a man who will go halfway to meet an old friend who wants to make up after a quarrel. We will deliver the charcoal."

Luis had seen enough of life to know that grown men sometimes act like children. These men were too old to have a silly quarrel that kept the charcoal-seller from delivering an order. But Luis had known such things to happen before. He took it simply as his own good luck and asked no questions.

Charcoal comes in pieces about the size of the end of your finger. It is pretty—glossy black, yet soft-looking. But it is the smudgiest stuff you can find. By the time he had held two sacks while the man shoveled charcoal into them, Luis's face and shirt were good and dirty.

As he shoveled, the charcoal-seller talked in a voice as sad as his mustache. "Most of the rich ones who live on this street are now using gas to cook with. One day a stove will blow up and smash a whole family to bloody little pieces. Then we will see how they like their shiny new stoves! But Doña Josefa has as much good sense as she has money. Charcoal was good enough for her father and grandfather, and it's good enough for her!"

The charcoal-seller fastened a sack of charcoal to Luis by a band that went around his forehead. The sack was nearly as big as Luis himself. With his back bent under it, he looked like an ant struggling with a twig. The charcoal-seller took up his own sack and they shuffled across to Doña Josefa's, walking with bent, springy knees the way we Mexicans do when we carry heavy weights. The charcoal-seller said good morning to the man beside the door. Luis kept his head down. He was anxious all the while they waited for the door to

open. He kept telling himself that the man could not do anything to him if he did recognize him. But Luis could not stop being frightened.

At last the door opened. With his eyes on the ground, Luis shuffled inside. As the door shut behind him, there broke out a wild screaming that seemed to come from all around the patio. Luis raised his head so suddenly that the carrying band cut into him and hurt. Then he grinned, for the screamers were parrots. There must have been a dozen of them, some on perches, some in big cages.

The patio was very large and had a small grove of orange and lime trees in the middle. The archways that ran around all four sides were so filled with vines and bushes that Luis could not see into the porch behind them. The main difference between this house and most others Luis had been in was that this one had two stories.

The charcoal-seller went shuffling across the patio. Luis followed. As they drew near the porch at the rear, two maids came out, giving cries of surprise. "Juanito!" they called. "Juanito, your friend the charcoal-seller has come."

The parrots screamed so that Luis did not know whether the cook answered or not. One of the maids opened the door of a storeroom off the kitchen. Luis eased the sack of charcoal to the floor and touched his forehead where the carrying band had hurt it. His fingers came away bloody from a spot where the skin had been rubbed off. Hearing voices in the kitchen, he went to peer around the charcoal-seller, who stood in the doorway talking with the two maids.

Luis had never seen such a kitchen. The stove ran nearly the width of the room; there were no less than eight separate holes where pots could be set over charcoal fires. The front of the stove was covered with a picture made of bright, gleaming tiles in four colors. The picture showed the tall, thin knight named Don Quixote and his fat servant, Sancho Panza. They are the main people in the most famous book ever written in Spain. In all countries where Spaniards have lived, one finds their pictures.

The tiles went clear to the ceiling, making a pale-red, shining wall. Colored tiles like those of the picture were set here and there to form designs. More beautiful still were the gleaming copper pots and pans that hung like ornaments against this wall.

As Luis stood staring into the kitchen, Juanito the cook came in through another door. The charcoal-seller said in his sad voice that it was kind of the cook to send a boy to help carry the charcoal, but why had Juanito not come himself?

"Boy?" said the cook. "What boy? Where is he?"

He said this so loudly that Luis heard, even though he was already running toward the trees in the center of the patio. He worked his way quickly through them and into the thick bushes and vines that screened the archways of the porch. Luis does not lose his head easily. As he went, he gave the house a good looking-over. The pillars of the porch were carved all over with fruit and leaves. There was more carving on the upper balcony. He decided that he did not like this house as much as ours. It was more rich than beautiful.

All the while Luis was making his way through the leaves, the parrots kept up a racket. One of them was shouting over and over, "Snow! Snow! Fresh ices and snow!" This is the cry of a certain old man who comes through our *barrio* selling ice cream from a pushcart.

Luis was so startled he nearly fell down when a voice just in front of him said clearly and impatiently, "Be quiet, General! You old fool!"

"Don't you love me, darling? Awrk, awrk, awrk!" said the parrot.

CHAPTER 6

The Adventure at Doña Josefa's

Men laughed beyond the vines. Luis, moving a little closer, looked between the leaves. In comfortable chairs, three men sat around a small table in the coolness of the porch. One was a large Yankee with hair the color of straw and blue eyes. One was a lean, smooth-looking man whose expensive suit matched the pale brown of his half-bald head. The third was Don Arturo Amador.

The parrot stopped his nonsense, and the men went back to their talk. It nearly drove Luis crazy with curiosity. To be so close to an important talk between men and not to be able to understand! He strained his ears trying to catch one or two of the English words he had learned in school. It was no use. All he got to satisfy his curiosity was some idea of what they were like.

The Yankee had a slow, quiet smile. He spoke little. His big hands rested quietly on the table. His blue eyes always looked into the face of the person who was speaking.

The man with the half-bald head had a narrow face with a large nose. His eyes were very large, also. He lounged back in his chair and seemed very much at home. When he spoke, his long, narrow hands made graceful motions. Often the others laughed at what he said. By the way he looked and spoke, this man made himself seem above the other two. He seemed to be doing them a favor by sitting at the table with them.

This bothered Luis, because he did not see how there could be a grander person than Arturo Amador. When he rode in processions, his black *charro** costume glittered with silver, and he sat his horse so gracefully and managed him with such skill that few men could compare with him. He had fought in the ring as an amateur bullfighter. He had flown his own private plane for a while. He had eyes like black stars, white teeth, and a well-muscled, slender body that would

---

* *Charros* are Mexico's best horseback riders. You will hear more about them later on.

never put on fat. Arturo Amador looked the way the Mexican people think Mexicans should look. He was everything Luis admired.

Many others—both men and women—admired him also. His family had been well known in Guadalajara for a long, long time. Up until the Revolution, the Amadors had been rich. But they had lost much of their land and other wealth during the troubled times that lasted very long in the State of Jalisco. Arturo Amador did not like being poor, so he began to make money from the sports he loved so much. Two ranches had been left to him because they had been losing money and no one wanted them. On one of these he began to raise fighting bulls; on the other he bred horses. He was what you call in the United States a sports promoter, making money from bullfights, horse races, and boxing matches and other sports. Don Arturo's name was often seen in the papers and often heard over the radio. When he came to his seat at a bullfight or a baseball game, people in the crowd pointed him out to one another. "That is Don Arturo Amador," they said. "He has a thousand friends, and they are all glad to do him favors."

As he listened to the three men, Luis learned that the person with the half-bald head was named Señor Pidal. The blond North American was Mr. Johnson. But Luis did not find out why they were here in Doña Josefa's house. In fact, no one—except Señor Pidal—knew the whole reason until much later. If Luis had known what was in Pidal's mind, he would have slipped away at once. Because he did not know, his curiosity was greater than his fear, so he stayed there gawking. Mr. Johnson would not have been there at all if he had known what Pidal was plotting.

Mr. Johnson, though quite young, was the owner of a big glass factory in the United States. He had come to Mexico on a vacation. Naturally he made the trip to Guadalajara to see how we make our famous blue and green glass, which is used in many homes in California. Many days he spent watching our workmen. They blow through long pipes into gobs of glass they dip out of glowing furnaces. As they blow, the melted glass puffs out like red-hot soap bubbles. The men turn it, twist it, press it against molds, and finally set it in ovens where it cools slowly.

"This is wonderful!" Mr. Johnson thought. "It would be a great loss if the people should stop making glass by hand. But cups and plates and vases are not the only things we use glass for nowadays. Mexico is changing—changing. The people want the same things we want in the United States."

Mr. Johnson thought of refrigerators—with their walls stuffed with glass threads to keep the heat from coming in. He thought of factories, with glass pipes to carry liquids which eat through iron and brass. He thought of eyeglasses and telescopes and microscopes; of bottles and tubes in hospitals for testing blood and giving "shots";

of windows that let in every ray of light, and windows which one can see into but cannot see out of. These and hundreds of other things of glass are best made by machinery, in factories.

"Why not start a factory here?" Mr. Johnson said to himself. "Guadalajara is just the place for a glass factory."

Mr. Johnson had no sooner thought this than he reached for the telephone in his hotel room. He called the one man in Guadalajara whom he knew. This was Señor Pidal.

Mr. Johnson had met Pidal at dinner with some wealthy friends in Mexico City. Pidal, they said, was a Spaniard. He seemed to know many important people, both in Mexico and in Europe. He seemed also to be making important business deals all the time. Mr. Johnson's friends did not say what these deals were. There was something mysterious about Pidal that made him seem more important and more interesting still.

Mr. Johnson said later that if he had been at home he would not have talked over his plans with Pidal without finding out more about the man. Being a stranger in a strange land, he was not so careful. When one is lonely—as Mr. Johnson was—it is easy to feel friendly toward people who are nice to you.

Pidal was very nice to Mr. Johnson. He took him out to the country club to play golf, and

entertained him in other ways. The plan to build
a glass factory seemed very good, Pidal said. But
he said that it would be very hard to get the
government to allow him to build the factory and
start a company. It would be impossible for Mr.
Johnson to do anything himself, Pidal said. To get
the factory started, he would need an agent—
someone who knew the Mexicans and their ways.

Pidal let Mr. Johnson understand that there
were many tricks that must be used. He made it
seem, almost, that the Mexicans would have to
be fooled into allowing the factory to be built.
A good deal of money would have to be spent in
ways that must be kept secret. Pidal strongly
hinted that the man to get the business started
for Mr. Johnson and spend Mr. Johnson's money
was—Señor Pidal himself.

Pidal had asked Arturo Amador to invite them
to Doña Josefa's house for two reasons. He

wanted Mr. Johnson to think that Don Arturo would help him with the glass factory business. He wanted also to show the picture-book side of life in Mexico—the old-fashioned kind, with big *haciendas** and big houses. He thought that this would put Mr. Johnson in a good mood.

* *Haciendas* were very large farms. In the old days, some were so big that they had whole villages within their borders. The owners were very rich and lived like dukes or princes.

As I said, Luis knew none of this as he stood there trying to puzzle out the English words flying back and forth between the three men. And Mr. Johnson thought that Pidal was a friendly, pleasant, amusing man who would help him build a glass factory. But Arturo Amador was beginning to have suspicions.

Suddenly he leaned forward, looking very hard at Pidal. "I would hate to think, *señor*," he said in Spanish, "that you were trying to trick somebody out of his money."

For just a second Señor Pidal's eyelids dropped low over his large eyes. He gave Don Arturo a look Luis did not understand—until later, when he found out that it was a look of hatred. Then Pidal smiled pleasantly and started to speak.

Whatever he said was drowned out by a woman's shriek from above.

"There he is! There he is! There behind the lime tree, among the vines. Catch him, Juanito!"

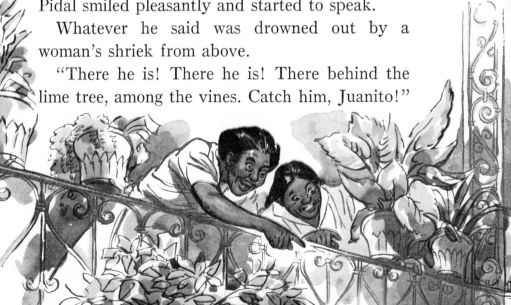

Looking up, Luis saw the heads of two of the maids, looking down from the second-story balcony. The branches and vine leaves hid Luis from everyone on the ground, but made no covering above him. They had spotted him easily.

He heard the cook crashing among the branches behind him, and whirled, ready to dart away. If it had not been for Arturo Amador, he would have escaped. With one leap Don Arturo left his place, broke through the vines, caught Luis by the arm, and dragged him onto the porch. Don Arturo's words came sharp, like the slap of a fist struck into the palm of one's hand. "Who are you? Why are spying on us? What do you want?"

Señor Pidal was smiling in a way that made Luis remember that he was smudged all over with charcoal. When Pidal turned and said something amusing in English to Mr. Johnson, Luis felt as if he wanted to sink through the tile floor. "Please," he said. "Please, Don Arturo! I will explain everything. But not here. They are laughing at me!"

Don Arturo looked at him hard for a moment. "Where do you come from?"

"My home is in the next street," answered Luis. "I belong in this *barrio*."

Don Arturo nodded as if partly satisfied, and led Luis down the porch, out of hearing. Luis had now gotten his breath back. He decided that the only thing to do was tell Don Arturo the truth. But since it was surprising to a grownup that a boy should take so much trouble to find out about a house just so it could be copied in a clay model, Don Arturo asked many sharp questions. Finally, Luis said, "There was also the adventure of it, *señor*. Everybody said I couldn't get in, and the man at the door warned me away. So I had to come in to show that I could. Didn't you ever do anything just for the adventure, Don Arturo?"

A new look came into Don Arturo's black eyes. "That is one of the best reasons I know of," he said, and took Luis back to where the others were sitting.

"This is a neighborhood boy," he explained. "He's a nervy little rascal, but he doesn't mean any harm."

Don Arturo had forgotten himself and talked in Spanish. Now he broke off and explained what

Luis had done, in English so Mr. Johnson could understand.

"Now," he said, turning to Luis and speaking in Spanish once more, "run along and do not use your talent for getting into places where you don't belong. It's likely to land you in jail."

"Yes, sir," said Luis. "Thank you very much."

Señor Pidal rose gracefully to his feet. "I'll just walk to the door with him," he said. "Manuel, my chauffeur, takes good care that no one bothers me. He might be a little rough with this boy. Manuel will be angry because the youngster got into the house after he told him to stay out."

Señor Pidal kept their pace slow as they walked across the patio by a path leading among the trees. He asked what Luis's father did for a living, and how Luis liked going on trips with the burros, and several other things. He seemed so friendly and interested that Luis began to like him. Just as they reached the big street door, Señor Pidal took out his wallet and handed Luis a card which had his address and telephone number printed under his name.

"If you should want a job," he said, "come to see me. I could use a boy like you. I promise you more excitement than you have working for your father. And the pay will be the pay of a man."

The maid opened the door. Manuel was still leaning against the wall. He seemed surprised to see them.

"This is Luis," said Señor Pidal. "He will be coming to work for me, I think. I want you to remember him, and treat him well. *Adiós* (good-by), Luis."

When the door closed, Luis hurried away. For the look he got from Manuel was most unfriendly.

CHAPTER 7

My Father Decides

Isabela, our cook, always managed to forget something when she went to the market early in the morning. It is the Mexican way to buy little packages of food which last for only a few meals. Housewives and maids shop every day. I do not know why our people shop in this way, but I know that Isabela liked it. Going to market gave her a chance to talk to her friends and hear all the news of the neighborhood. She liked it so much that she always had to go back in the afternoon for something she had not remembered in the morning.

On the day when Luis found the three men in Doña Josefa's house, Isabela came waddling in from her afternoon trip just as I was going back to work on the model. I had worked hard all morning. The house next door was done, and I had begun to work on the one next to that. The new plan—and Luis—had put new life into me. I felt better than I had felt at any time since I got sick.

I suppose that my family spoiled me a good deal. I seem to have been given most of the things I asked for, all my life. At the time I am telling you of—when I was ten—I had not learned to be patient. That afternoon I wanted Luis to come. It was lonesome working by myself, and I wanted to hear about his adventures.

When Isabela stopped beside our model, I told her about this—calling Luis slowpoke and false friend and other names. Isabela laughed so that her three brown chins quivered. She said, "If you get impatient waiting for Luis, you will wear yourself to a shadow. He is one of those who says to himself, 'My friend is doing what he is doing. Why should I stop what I am doing just because we are supposed to get together at this time?' But Luis will always come—and when he comes you will know it was worth while to wait. For what he has been doing will make a fine, interesting story. I have had two husbands like that."

Isabela rolled on toward the kitchen, still shaking with laughter.

It is hard for a boy to make use of the wisdom of grownups. I am ashamed to say that I would have bitten all my fingernails off with impatience, except that a wonderful thing happened. My father asked me to go with him to church.

"You seem much better, Martín," he said. "And I would very much like to have you come with your mother and me. I have a special reason."

I must explain to you that in Guadalajara going to church is as important a part of a child's life as playing. We are taken when we are very young—and not on Sundays only. Many people go every day to pray in church. I had felt very uncomfortable all the while since I took sick because I could not go to church. And I had been looking forward to the time when Our Lady of Zapopan would come to our *barrio*. Her home is a big church in a small town nearby, and she comes to Guadalajara each summer and visits around, spending a few days in each of our churches. When she leaves one to go to another, there is a procession. The richer the *barrio,* the more bright and wonderful the procession. Our *barrio* has fine ones, with *charros* on beautiful horses and dancers wearing masks who whirl and leap to music of instruments made by putting strings across armadillo shells. My parents had promised that I could go and see Our Lady of

Zapopan come to our *barrio*. She would come soon, but I was glad of this chance to get out sooner.

We went in the bigger of our two cars, with Anselmo driving, though the church is only a few blocks from our house.

The outside of our church is not beautiful. It is made of dull-colored, smooth stone and looks rather like a castle. In front of it there is a stone-paved courtyard, with a high iron fence at the edge of the sidewalk. One time, soldiers camped

in that courtyard and people fought them from inside the church. But many other things have happened in and around that church, things that never get into history books because they are important to only a few people. But how important to those few!

Our parents bring us to this church to be baptized and confirmed. Most boys and girls of the *barrio* expect to be married there. We come there to pray for the souls of those we have loved and who are now dead. We come there also to ask God's help in making up our minds about important things.

My father was very quiet and wrapped up in himself. As he got out of the car it seemed to me that he was more lost in his own thoughts than usual. My mother kept glancing at him, as if she wondered what went on in his mind. She was wearing a dark-blue dress with big white flowers on it. Over her head she had a long shawl of very thin cloth. It was black. Several other women who came out of the church were wearing shawls that way—like mantillas. It made them look Spanish. But my mother, beautiful though she is, seemed more like the women with *rebozos*

84

wrapped round their shoulders and tucked under their arms.

I do not quite know what it is that makes my mother look un-Spanish. Her father—the General—was half Tarascan. The Tarascans are an old people who were rich and great in Mexico before the Spaniards came. My mother shows that she is the General's daughter—but one cannot say exactly how.

We went across the courtyard to the church, and I was very much excited. It had been so long since I was out among the people of Guadalajara! It was even exciting to hear the sounds of many feet. There were the slap-slap sounds of *guaraches* (sandals) worn by poor workingmen in grimy white trousers and peaked straw hats. There were clicking sounds of high-heeled shoes worn by girls. There were squeaky sounds that came from the old-fashioned shoes with buttons that Don Leopoldo insists on wearing. He has been selling lime and plaster in our *barrio* since my father was a boy. He will not change his ways, and his shoes and his floppy summer clothes of white silk make him odd and old fashioned. People laugh at him, yet it is hard to think how Our Lady of Zapopan could be brought to our church without Don Leopoldo to manage things.

Many people spoke to us and asked after my health. It took us some while to get into the church.

It was a wonderful feeling. I do not know how I can describe it to you, the feeling of the people of our *barrio* kneeling all together and saying the answers of the prayer. Their voices went up and became one big voice in the curved ceiling of the church. The priest's deep voice went ahead of us, leading the way.

At first I could not see, because of coming from bright sunlight into dimness. But then I began to look around for things that had always made me happy. First, the two big, oval-shaped pictures high on the wall—the pictures of the miracle of Our Lady of Guadalupe showing herself to a poor, humble Aztec. Next, the high altar with the white,

white candles in their gold candlesticks. My eyes went all over the church while I said the prayer with my father and mother and crossed myself. I began to feel safe and comfortable in my heart— a way I had not felt since I first got sick.

You can feel people pray. You know when they are with you and when they are not. My mother and I were together, feeling the same feeling as we spoke the words. But my father was not with us, though he said the same things at the same time as we did. He was praying by himself, in a very solemn way. He was asking God something.

This was a prayer service, and people came and went as they chose. After about fifteen minutes my father looked down at my mother and we rose from our knees. Anselmo had the car waiting.

When we got into the house, my father put an arm around my mother and touched me on the shoulder. He guided us toward the library, which my father also uses as an office. But before we reached the door a voice called, "Martín! Martín!" and there came Luis running down the patio.

My father frowned, as if he did not want Luis around. Then he laughed and said to my mother,

"It does not seem so solemn a thing, now that God has helped me to make up my mind. I wanted to share this first of all with my wife and son, but there is no reason why Luis should not hear it also. His life seems to be twining around ours like a vine. What I wish to say is that I have decided to be mayor of Guadalajara if the people will have me."

My mother hugged my father's arm, looking very glad. But I was puzzled.

"What took you so long to decide?" I asked. "I don't see any reason why you would not want to be mayor."

"A man whom the people elect to an important place in their government is always blamed for everything that goes wrong," my father said. "Also, many people want things they should not have. Other people want to do things they should not do. It is the government's business to stop such people from doing wrong.

"If I become mayor I shall make many enemies, and they will not care what they say about me. George Washington, the first President of the United States and 'Father of His Country,' was called a traitor and worse by his enemies.

That is one reason why he refused to be president more than twice. That is why many Mexicans who are well-educated men and would make good governors and mayors and presidents will not try to get these offices. This is why I asked God whether it is best for me to be mayor. Today, in the *templo* (temple), He let me see that a man must not step aside from such a duty. Rather, he should go to meet it."

Luis stood there looking as if he would fight anyone who spoke badly of my father. My mother changed the subject.

"And did you get into Doña Josefa's house, Luis?" she asked, smiling.

So Luis began to tell us. My parents found the story so interesting that we sat down and had *refrescos* (cool, refreshing drinks) while he told everything that happened.

Toward the end, my father grew very thoughtful. "Pidal!" he said. "What is it I heard in Mexico City about this Pidal? It is in my mind that what I heard is not good. That is the trouble with Arturo Amador's business. He meets many people who make their living by gambling on sports—and they are not always good people."

"Señor Pidal seems like a fine gentleman," Luis said. "You can tell that he is very rich and high up in the world, yet he was kind to me."

"Perhaps I remember wrong," said my father. "Go and work on your model, *hijos* (sons). If you know what you want, you can go downtown tomorrow and buy some figures of people to put in the streets. Martín seems well enough."

CHAPTER 8

Things That "Sell Themselves Crying"

If we had gone downtown the next morning, as we had planned, Luis would not have worn his green sweater. It was a hot, bright morning. Without Luis's green sweater to start them off, the things that began happening on the day after, when we did go downtown, would never have begun.

These things matter more than anything that has happened to Luis in his whole life, up to now. So Luis's green sweater is important—like the nail that was missing from the king's horse-shoe.* In Guadalajara things often happen because of some accident—like a rainstorm or a blown-out tire, or a hole in a sweater. In the United States you manage so well that things

---

* For want of a nail, the shoe was lost.
  For want of a shoe, the horse was lost.
  For want of a horse, the kingdom was lost.

happen just as they are supposed to, and right on time. Or do they?

The reason we did not go downtown that day was that a letter came from our aunt in the city of Torreón. The letter invited my sister to visit our aunt for a month. Torreón is very gay, because the people make a lot of money growing cotton. My sister would go to a lot of parties, then go with the family to stay on their big cattle ranch in the mountains of Durango. I was jealous of my sister, I am ashamed to say.

Lucía had been staying with some friends out in the newest part of Guadalajara, to be near the tennis club during the tournament. In the old parts of the city, where everything is built up, there is very little room for tennis courts and playgrounds.

My mother sent for Lucía. She sent also for Señora Castelar, the sewing woman who lived not far from Luis. There was a bizz, buzz, buzz of woman-talk and the three of them disappeared into the sewing room and did not come out.

I felt quite left out of things until Luis came. Then we became very busy on the model. I had finished the house next door and it was time to decide what we would do next. The most important things about Doña Josefa's house were the second story—which we could show by making the walls and porches of the patio—and the kitchen. My mother said that we must show people what a beautiful thing an old-fashioned Spanish kitchen could be. While we were talking about it, I had a really good idea.

"I've got an old kaleidoscope in my room," I said to Luis. "We'll take the little pieces of colored glass and set them into the walls and the stove to make designs."

Luis slapped me on the shoulder. "Wonderful!" he said. "We can't make the picture of Don Quixote out of the glass, but it will look pretty. Maybe we can find some little copper pots and pans downtown."

It seemed to us that we did not need to make the rooms of any of the other houses in our block. It would give a good idea of how the block looked if we made the walls along the street, with places cut in for doors and windows. We could leave spaces for patios, with plain walls around them. Over the parts where the rooms were supposed to be, we could put boards painted red, for roofs.

Luis took some chalk and marked out the walls of the *vecindad* where he lived. We planned to make the block where the *vecindad* was, and also the block across the street from my house. These would be just walls with doors and windows along the streets, and boards for roofs, except that we were going to make one of the stores. The one we chose was on the corner. Behind it were rooms where the storekeeper and his family lived. It is so hard to put things like this into words that I will have to draw you a plan to show how this store-home looked. Many people in Guadalajara live in such places.

Together, Luis and I marked out spaces for the garden and the *barrio* church. We planned also to make the *barrio* market and the stable where Luis's father kept his animals. But we knew that we would not get to those for a while.

When we had gotten everything planned out, Luis began to get restless. It is very hard for Luis to stay in any one place for long at a time. He kept looking toward the door, as if he wished he could think of some excuse for getting out. But he did not think of any until my father came home. In Guadalajara we usually have dinner in the middle of the afternoon. My father often comes home about noon and works in his library until dinner is served. In this way he is like Luis—he enjoys moving around. I guess that most people in Guadalajara are restless and have a hard time staying in one place.

As soon as he came home, my father stopped by the model to see how things were getting along. We showed him the chalk lines marking places where buildings would be and explained our plan. My father was very pleased with the *vecindad;* he said it was good to show all the ways people live. But he asked, "Are you sure you have chosen the most important places in the *barrio?* Have you forgotten nothing?"

"I'll just go and make sure," Luis said. "I'll make a list of every place that people use in their lives around here."

Before I could say anything, he grabbed up his battered straw hat and ran across the patio, calling, "Anselmo, open the door for me, please!"

I worked for a while, but the left-out feeling began to come back. It was worse after dinner, because my sister Lucía kept talking to Mother about her trip and her new clothes. My father finished eating quickly and left.

Instead of working on the model after I had my rest, I moped around the house feeling sorry for myself. I took the glass out of the old kaleidoscope. And then I brought some comic books out of my room and sat down at the table on the porch to read. The comic books seemed dull. It was not long after this that I gave up reading them altogether. After a while I put my head down on my arms, a very sad boy.

I felt a soft arm come to rest across my shoulders and heard my mother's voice ask what was the matter. I do not remember what I told her—

the way I felt seems silly to me, now. But she understood very quickly, the way mothers do.

"Come," she said, and led me into the *sala*. She made me sit on the window ledge where I could see up the street and down the street. It was filled with afternoon sunshine so bright that the buildings seemed almost to quiver. No one at all was on the street except a man coming slowly down our block with some tall bamboo poles over his shoulder. At the ends of the poles were feathers, so he looked as if he were carrying some great, crazy bird out of a fairy story. I began to smile, for he turned toward the houses from time to time and cried out in a loud voice, as if the bird were prancing and screaming.

"I had forgotten how funny the *plumeros* (feather-sellers) look," I said.

"But we need them," said my mother. "How would we ever dust the walls and ceilings of these high, old-fashioned houses unless we had feather dusters on long poles."

The *plumero* smiled at us, even though we had to tell him we did not want a duster today.

"Luis will bring back one picture of our *barrio*," my mother said. "But you and I can get another picture by simply looking out the window. We can get the view the women see. Long, long ago the Spaniards decided to keep their women shut up in the house as much as possible. The Aztecs and other people who lived in Mexico before the Spaniards came also made their women stay close at home. It is no wonder

that this custom has lasted in Mexico clear down to our own time.

"What happened because the women were kept at home, you will see by watching our street. The women could not go out into the world, so the whole world came to the women."

It was true. After the *plumero* had passed, there came a young boy riding a bicycle with a tray balanced on his head. He was making deliveries to the little stores in our *barrio*. On a bicycle, riding fast, with a big tray on his head, a boy does not have much chance to look around. But this boy saw us and gave us a quick smile. A truck came rumbling by, and the truck driver slowed down to look at us and smile. Next came a man with a burro loaded with pineapples. Not many people who sell in the streets use burros

nowadays but there are a few. The pineapple-seller stopped in front of our window and told us a long story about his fruit. He said his were the very finest pineapples that grew in the low, hot lands along the coast of our State of Jalisco. He said that the man who raised them was a friend of his. It was not true, of course. His pineapples had come in a railroad car with thousands of others. But it was a good story. My mother laughed and told the man to go to the front door. Then she sent me to ask Isabela if we needed pineapples, and there was more talk at the front door while we bought some.

After this we went back to the window and talked with a man who sold cooked ears of corn from a pushcart. He knew that I had been sick and gave us some advice about how to get me strong. When he left, a shoemaker came along, one of those who goes from house to house mending shoes. A woman who lived in the house next door stopped and talked to my mother about plans for the procession of Our Lady of Zapopan. Don Porfirio, driving his red car, bowed to us. This made us laugh because he is so fat there is scarcely room for him to move once he gets behind the wheel.

100

So it went, until the sun began to fade from the street and shadows reached toward our windows from the houses opposite. I sat in the window long after Lucía called my mother to come and help her with the sewing. Everyone who passed had a quick look, a smile, a word to toss into our window.

I made a list—a list of all the things that are sold by people who come along our street crying their wares, the things, as we say in Spanish, that "sell themselves crying (*se venden gritando*)."

MARTÍN'S LIST OF THINGS SOLD IN THE STREETS

Brushes	Fruits
Dusters	Vegetables
Brooms	Flowers
Medicines	Nuts
Candy	Sweet drinks
Chewing gum	Extra-pure water
Ice cream	Sandwiches
Tarts	

Little statues of saints

Creams and other beauty aids

Food-drinks made of strained corn and flavored in several different ways

Corn on the cob (cooked)

Tacos (chopped meat, wrapped in *tortillas*)

Tostados (*tortillas* with cheese rolled up in them)

Gorditas ("little fat ones"—sweet, thick *tortillas* made of wheat)

Tamales (mixture of corn flour and meat wrapped in corn-husks)

LUIS'S LIST OF IMPORTANT PLACES IN THE BARRIO
WHERE HE AND MARTÍN LIVED

1 church	6 blacksmith shops
1 market	20 sewing women's workrooms
1 theater	20 *tortilla* factories
5 schools	2 ice cream factories
2 hospitals	15 charcoal-sellers' stalls
4 garages	7 drugstores
1 cemetery	6 carpenter shops
1 hall for prize fights	10 barbershops
8 plumbers' shops	10 beauty shops
12 shoe repair shops	1 taxi stand

4 places selling bricks and other building materials

1 stable for keeping burros and other animals for short times

5 factories making bedspreads and other household things on hand looms

30 stores (Most of the stores sell food and soft drinks, candy, candles, and other things for daily use. Some have handkerchiefs and other things to wear. A few sell no food, but have paint, tools, paper, string, and things of that kind. All these stores, even the smallest, are more like country general stores in the United States than like any of the other stores you are used to.)

CHAPTER 9

I Behave Very Badly

The next morning Luis came, wearing his green sweater. He had put out of his mind the big, ragged hole in the elbow, for he had no other sweater to wear on that rainy, colder-than-usual morning. I did not notice the hole—though of course the women did. He came while Rómulo and his mother were at our house. Rómulo noticed the hole, too.

My mother had promised me at breakfast that we would go downtown that morning. Luis and I could hunt for figures to go into our model, while my mother and Lucía went to a store which sold women's clothes brought all the way from France. Raquel, the daughter of the sewing woman, worked in this store. The sewing woman had gotten Lucía and my mother excited about some fancy things that had just come in.

I do not know what they were, though Lucía chattered about them all through breakfast. I was thinking about going downtown, where I had not been for two months. But then the telephone rang, and it seemed that it would be a long time before we got away.

An old school friend of my mother's had called from the airport. Her name was Natalia. She wanted to come for a visit that morning, bringing her son Rómulo.

Many friends stop to visit us. Guadalajara is near the center of Mexico, and because of this, airlines and highways and railways meet there as the spokes of a wheel meet at the hub. People traveling between Mexico City and the north stop in Guadalajara. People going to the west coast stop also. This makes a lot of business. It is one of the reasons why Guadalajara is a large, busy city. It is also one reason why we have the custom of being hospitable.

My family likes to have friends come—but this was not a good day to have Rómulo and his mother, Doña Natalia. She chattered and chattered as usual. My sister and I grew more and more restless and bored as we sat in the *sala* and listened to her. And I grew cross. My excuse is that I was not very well.

It is too bad that my mother chose this time to make a certain kind of mistake through which parents often get children into trouble. She turned to me and said, "Son, why don't you show Rómulo your model of Guadalajara? He is studying architecture at the University of Mexico and I'm sure he can give you some very good advice."

"A model of Guadalajara?" said Natalia, in a voice that went up like a fluttering bird. "In clay? How precious! Rómulo will be fascinated."

Rómulo said nothing, and neither did I. What I wished most in the world was to sink through the floor. Why is it that parents think that the children of their friends and relations will be interested in what their own children are doing? And why do they think that their own children always wish to share what they are doing with these children of friends? This is one of the things about parents I do not understand.

Rómulo was then a young man seventeen years old. He would be bored with looking at my model. I could tell by the way he fingered the small mustache on his lip. His face is too fat for a mustache, but one could tell he was proud of it. He felt too old for childish things like my model.

There was nothing to do but take him out to see it. Anselmo had let in Luis while we were in the *sala,* and he was already at work. Rómulo shook Luis's hand when I introduced them, but I saw his eyes go to the hole in Luis's sweater. A funny expression came on Rómulo's mouth, and he turned to the model.

Right then I began to get angry with him. I grew more angry still at the way he fingered his mustache and said, "Hmm! Hmm!" at the model. The funny expression on his mouth was a smile he was trying to hide. I could see that, because the smile grew bigger as he said, "Very nice—for boys of your age. Just get me a ruler, will you?"

I had to bring the ruler because he was a guest. He set it up beside the front wall of the model of our house, clamped down his thumb to mark the place, and moved the ruler to the back wall. "It's a whole inch and a half higher back here," he said. "Surely you boys can see how silly that is. Another thing—these arches around the patio are not the same width. And the pillars!" he almost laughed out loud. "This pillar is as thin as a pencil and the next one is as wide as my thumb. Now, if you will just take a little clay off the thick one—like this—and put it on the thin one—like that—you can easily——"

This was too much for me. "Get away from our model!" I said, giving him a push.

"Don't be a little fool!" said Rómulo, getting angry and stubborn. "I'm just trying to show you how to make it look halfway right."

He reached out toward the model again and I lost my head. Or rather, I used it in a wrong way. I ran at Rómulo and butted him in his soft stomach. He staggered back, holding part of an arch and a pillar which had come away in his hand.

There was a big mess. Rómulo's mother and my mother came out and I got scolded very hard and sent to my room. Luis hid in the kitchen with Isabela for fear someone would blame him for the trouble.

I was left alone in my room for a long time. I cried very hard—partly because of what Rómulo had done to the model, partly because my mother had scolded me, partly because I was a little ashamed—but mostly because I was mad.

I was lying face down on the bed when my father came in. He pulled me up and sat on the bed with his arm around me. He was angry with me, but I knew he would not punish me until he had heard my side of the story.

"Rómulo didn't have any business to touch our model!" I said when I had finished telling what had happened. "Maybe it isn't any good, but it's ours and we want to make it all ourselves. Nobody else should touch it but Luis and me."

My father looked at me quite a while before he answered. "Do not think you were right in being rude to Rómulo," he said. "One is always polite to a guest, no matter what he does. But I cannot punish you, Martín. Rómulo should not have touched the model. To do one's own work, on one's own projects, is a right that belongs to every child—and every man and woman. I am glad that you want to make Guadalajara for yourself. It is the things we do for ourselves that teach us the most and bring us most happiness in this life. You should not have butted Rómulo—but I cannot punish you for defending your rights."

My father then told me to wash my face and get ready to go downtown. So I did. Luis and my mother and my sister and I went in the big car, with Anselmo driving. My mother does not drive, and my father was taking the small car to go out into the country on business. Our cars are makes that you can see on every road in the United States. The parts are sent down from the United States and put together in our factories.

"Luis," I asked, as we drove away from our house, "what did my father say to you just before he left?"

Luis sat up straighter and looked important. "He said for me to keep my eyes and ears open and find out how people would feel about having him as mayor of Guadalajara. He said that I was good at finding out things. I suppose he thinks this because I learned that Arturo Amador has left the city."

"You did not tell me," I said, feeling a little left out.

"When did I have time?" asked Luis, throwing an arm around me. "I just heard it this morning when I stopped at the Cats for some candy. My old godmother never gives me anything to eat for breakfast but *tortillas* and coffee, and my father had me up at the crack of dawn to help him doctor a sick burro. A man gets hungry!"

Three blocks down from our house we passed some boys leaning out of a second-story window—which most houses here in Guadalajara do not have, as I said. They were letting down a clay *olla* (jar) on a rope to some other boys on the sidewalk.

"I know those boys," Luis said. "They are playing that the clay jar is a *piñata*.* They have a dream that somehow it will be filled with candy and all the children in the neighborhood will

---

* A *piñata* is a decorated earthenware pot or gourd filled with sweets. At Christmas and other festival times the *piñata* is broken and all the children share the sweets.

come to break the *piñata* at a fine party on the day of San Miguel, for whom the dark boy in the window is named. But the *piñata* will not be full and there will be no party. Miguel and his brother have no father, and the uncle with whom they live makes barely enough to feed his own family and them too. He works in a bank."

"It must be sad not to have a father," I said.

Luis glanced into the back seat, where my mother and Lucía were busy making their plans. "It is also a sad thing to have no mother," he said.

CHAPTER 10

We Go to the "Center"

Luis said that they looked like eyes. Lucía said that they looked like mouths opened wide in surprise. I said that the oval windows in the tall towers of the cathedral looked like windows and nothing more. Luis and Lucía and I fell to

113

arguing in this way as our car rolled slowly past the cathedral.

My mother said, "Whether they are mouths, eyes, or windows, you boys will have to make them. The cathedral is the center of Guadalajara."

She was right, of course. Our Mexican cities have grown the way a tree grows outward from its heart. In the center, the beginners of each city put a church—a cathedral much too big for its time. Beside the cathedral they left a big square. On the sides of this square they placed government buildings, palaces, and *portales,* which are wide porches where people buy and sell all sorts of things. As the cities grew, the streets around the cathedrals became streets of business. The outer "rings" of growth were added by people who did not care to live near this crowded, busy part, which we call *el Centro* (the Center).

Just beyond the cathedral, Anselmo had to stop because of a little accident. A taxi backed out from its place in the open square on one side of the cathedral. A carriage drawn by a black horse had come around from the other side, where a line of such carriages stands in front of a small, green park. The bumper of the taxi hooked the wheel of the carriage. Both drivers got out to shout at each other. A small crowd gathered.

Anselmo blew his horn, trying to get them to hurry up and unhook the bumper from the carriage wheel. But Lucía said, "Let them be, Anselmo. While we are stopped, Martín can have a good look at the *Zócalo* (the main square, or plaza, where we were). He will need to have the picture of it in his mind before he can build it in clay."

Sometimes my father teases Lucía and my mother by saying that the women of Guadalajara are so beautiful they could not possibly have any brains. The truth is that our women have bright minds as well as good looks. They are brave, too. It was a woman who put up the best fight against the Indians that came very close to wiping out Guadalajara in its earliest days. It was a woman who chose the place where the city now stands and persuaded the men to move there.

It was quite like Lucía to turn without warning from talk of clothes to talk of our model. She is a bright girl and she loves Guadalajara. She began telling us that we had to make all of the buildings near the *Zócalo*—the museum, which once was a convent; the federal building, where the post office and telegraph office are; and the *palacio* (palace) of the state government.

"I get excited every time I look at the *palacio*," Lucía said. "Father Hidalgo, sitting at a writing desk in that building, freed the slaves of Mexico many years before Lincoln freed the slaves in the United States. And it was in the *palacio* that some bad soldiers were about to kill President Juárez when the poet what's-his-name saved him."

116

"You would make a fine *profesora* (teacher) of history, *señorita*," Luis said, smiling back at Lucía.

"But it really is exciting to think of the things that have happened in these places we know so well! Building Guadalajara is the most wonderful idea I ever heard of. I'm so proud of you boys!"

Lucía has eyes like my father's, very dark, and set deep under eyebrows like a blackbird's feathers. When her eyes are lighted up, the way they were just then, she seems beautiful. One forgets that her nose is a little too big and her mouth too small. Like my father, she is rather serious and speaks straight from her heart. It made Luis and me happy to hear Lucía praise us for our work.

The taxi had been untangled from the carriage. Anselmo drove on—but slowly because of the trucks and automobiles and carts that flowed around us. I had plenty of time to look into the *portales* beside the big square.

"Please," I said. "Please let Luis and me get out and walk through the *portales*. We can meet you somewhere."

I had missed walking in the *portales* as much as anything—except church, perhaps—during the months I had been sick. As I said before, we people of Guadalajara love the sun. We love to move around. More than anything else, we love doing things together. For these reasons, we love the *portales*, and thousands go there every day. The sun shines through the archways, but one is sheltered from the heat. Between the pillars are stands selling everything from *sarapes* (hand-woven woolen blankets worn by men) to soda water. A man may stop to buy a toy for his child, move on to turn the leaves of books in an outdoor bookstore; stop for a *taco* and start on, munching and thinking, "Now I will go back to my office." Before he has reached the corner he meets a couple of friends. They stop to chat,

have a bottled drink. Before they have parted they may have done some business together.

Those of us who live in Guadalajara almost always meet friends in the *portales*. But even a lonely soul is not exactly alone. For every kind of person moves through the *portales*. The factory owner in a suit made by the best tailor touches elbows with a village woman wrapped in an old *rebozo* that almost hides her brown, weather-beaten face. The bullfighter makes himself smaller to let a priest go by. A gay and smiling lady stops short to keep from being run into by a child whose hands and face are already sticky with the candy he has just bought. To every-one—citizen and stranger, young or old, lucky or unfortunate—the ever-moving crowd in the *portales* seems to say, "Come, enjoy yourself with us!"

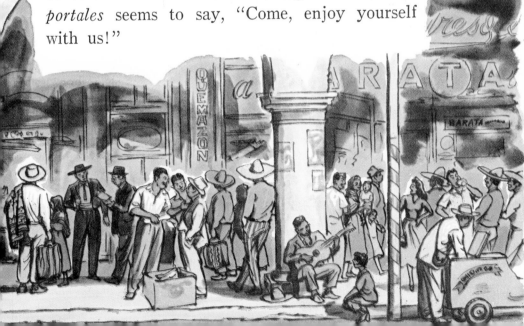

My mother knew well enough why I wanted to get out and walk in the *portales*.

But she would not let me. We drove on, past the new store that rises up shining and huge among the older buildings, across Juárez Avenue, and stopped before one of the French stores. There were blouses and *sevillanas* (small, fancy scarves that women wear on their heads) and other things in the windows—all so thin that the sunlight came through them. Lucía and my mother got out quickly.

Anselmo knows the city well. So does Luis. Because they knew where to go, we were able to look through a lot of stores, considering the time we had. Most of these stores were small, and sold other things, such as jewelry, or pictures of saints, along with the little figures we were looking for.

Most of the stores in Guadalajara are small compared with the downtown stores in the United States. I know that they seem cluttered to many people who come here from your country. But all of them are full of surprises, and many have very beautiful things. For hundreds of years goods have been coming to Guadalajara from all the countries of Europe, and from China and Japan also. We have many people who want only the best and most beautiful things that can be had, and our storekeepers try to please their fancies.

That day it was more fun to shop than usual because I had not done it for so long. We bought a man whom I could turn into a *plumero* by putting sticks with feathers in the curve of his arm. We bought a loaded burro, and a man to lead him. Also a push-cart man, a horse-cart, trucks, automobiles, and some men and women in ordinary clothes. I mean men in pants and shirts and *guaraches,* and women with *rebozos* and scarves over their heads. Women in Guadalajara seldom wear hats, but they usually have some pretty piece of cloth to go over their heads in case they want to go to church.

I wanted very much to find a fat woman like Isabela to go into the kitchen of our house. But I could not find any. Luis would not go into the last store where I searched for this figure. When I came out, I found him down the street, with his forehead pressed against a window.

He was staring at a saddle. He stood with lips a little parted, and I knew by his look that he was lost in a dream. The saddle had cost months of hard, patient work by very skillful hands. The design which ran all over it was so beautifully carved that it looked as if a rider had passed under thick-leaved trees and the pattern of light and shadow had printed itself on the leather. The horn was shining silver. The *conchas* (decorations of silver in the form of shells) sprinkled over the saddle were as big as silver dollars. Even the fringe hanging down from the covered stirrups was tipped with silver.

"Some day," said Luis, still in his dream, "I'm going to have a saddle like that and ride in the procession of Our Lady of Zapopan as a *charro*."

It surprised me a little that Luis thought he could ride well enough to be a *charro*. The men and boys who take goods on burros must walk.

"My uncle has a small ranch," Luis went on. "I was born there, and I learned to ride as soon as I learned to walk. One time, when I was very, very small, my father bought me a *charro* outfit. I was so proud, Martín! I sat my scraggly pony as if he had been the finest horse in Don Arturo Amador's stable—and I Don Arturo himself."

Luis pressed his nose against the glass and said softly, "My father promised to get me a new *charro* outfit as soon as I outgrew the first—and another when I outgrew that. But luck has not been with us." Luis put his hand on my shoulder and smiled, shaking the sadness from him. "Who knows? I may have my *charro* outfit sooner than I expect. The rich Señor Pidal has promised me a job. Maybe I'll get rich quickly, Martín."

I do not think that Luis meant what he said. He did not really intend to work for Señor Pidal—not then. He was simply chewing the idea to see how it tasted.

Anselmo, who had driven around the block so as not to park in the narrow street, blew the horn at us and we ran to get in. On our way to pick up my mother and Lucía, we drove once more past the new store. I stuck my head out the window (I know I shouldn't have) to look up at its height. Big as it is, and up-to-date as it is, it fits beautifully with the old buildings near it. The new store seemed already to belong to Guadalajara as if we had had it always.

"Maybe we should put the new store into our model," I said. "Everything we've planned so far is an old thing. We ought to have something new."

Luis laughed. "You were complaining about our planning too much just a little while ago!"

"It's true we can't make everything we'd like to," I said. "Let's talk it over with my father. He can help us decide."

Luis went into the French store to see if my mother and sister were ready. He came out with a load of packages. With him came a young woman, also with packages. She put them into the car tenderly, as if she loved the clothes my mother had bought for Lucía. I knew her, but I could not place her for a minute.

She was tall and not at all fat but not skinny either. She had very curly black hair going back from her forehead. And her face was shaped like the faces you see in some church pictures, like a heart, though narrower at the top and fuller at the bottom. But it was not a serious, saintly face. She was laughing with Luis, and you could see that she enjoyed life and was happy most of the time.

As they came closer, I knew it was Raquel, the daughter of the woman who has done sewing for my mother and Lucía ever since I can remember. I had seen Raquel many times. She and her mother lived around the corner from our house. Both had to work because Raquel's father had died when she was still a girl.

My mother says that our meeting with Raquel was the best and most important part of the adventure with Luis. This I do not believe—but a girl might easily think so.

Raquel asked me how I felt and said how sorry she was to think of my illness. It made me feel better to have her talk to me in this way, and to see her smile. My strength had not all come back in me, and I had begun to feel a little faint and unhappy. But Raquel made me feel good again—I do not know just how.

My mother and sister came soon and stood talking with Raquel about the clothes. When they had finally gotten into the car and Luis was about to follow, Raquel took his arm. She stood for a minute looking down at the big hole torn in the sleeve of his green sweater. Then she gave his arm a little shake, and smiled a small smile that was a little sad. *"Pobrecito!* (Poor youngster!)" she said. "Your godmother has gotten too old to look after you, Luis. This evening come to my house and I will mend your sweater for you. A boy who goes with the Mendosas should not have holes in his clothes."

CHAPTER 11

Raquel Asks for an Egg

"My father has eggs on his mind," said Luis, giving me a quick grin. "For this reason, I keep out of his way."

We were in the bathroom, washing up after a hard afternoon's work on the model. I had asked Luis how it came that his father left him so much free time to work with me. He had explained that the burros were worn out by the long trip into the mountains of Michoacán. They needed a rest. And so, as Luis said with a laugh, the man and boy got a rest, too.

Luis told me also how it was with himself and his father. They liked one another. But they saw so much of one another when they were out with the burros that when they were in the city they went their separate ways. When I asked Luis if his father did not keep track of him (as my family

127

certainly kept track of me), Luis's eyes danced more than ever.

"Martín," he said, "you are one of the fine, expensive horses of this world. Boys like you are turned out to graze in green pastures—with fences around them. Your families see to it that you are safe in the stable each night. Boys like me are life's burros. We are turned loose on the *campo* (range) to look out for ourselves. When the grownups want us, they round us up. Most of the time we come right along. But sometimes we make ourselves hard to find."

Luis then told me about his father having eggs on his mind. It sounded so odd that I thought he must be joking. But he was not.

"My father thinks that his best chance to make money is with eggs. He buys them cheap in little, out-of-the-way towns from housewives who want a few *centavos* (cents) to spend on market day. There are no highways to these towns. Some we reach by roads a *carreta* (cart with two high, solid wheels cut from a log) could not get through. My father says that if he had a truck to meet the burros at the highway and take the eggs on into the city, he would get rich."

We had been walking across the patio toward the front door as Luis told me this. He stopped suddenly and made a face.

"I hate eggs!" he said. "You spend for them all the money you have; you pack them with dry grass as if they were so many jewels. You balance the load as if you were weighing gold, so that there is just exactly the same weight on each side of the burro. You drive the animals along slowly, slowly, feeling all the time as if you were walking on the eggs. Suppose then that something frightens the burros. One bumps into another. What have you got for your money and your trouble? Scrambled eggs!"

Luis laughed, but only for a moment. His face was serious as he said, "What truly worries me is that my father will talk himself into another trip soon. Then I will not be able to work with you on the model or find out for your father how the people would like him for mayor of Guadalajara. I think——" he said slowly, and began to frown. "I think I will not go along if my father starts too soon."

"You would not dare to disobey your father," I said.

Luis gave me another grin. "Remember I am a burro myself, Martín. *Hasta mañana!* (Until tomorrow!)"

It was Don Bartolo's little boy who caused Luis to let it be known where he was going when he left the *vecindad* just after sunset. As he came, clean and with his hair shining wet, from the bathhouse, he could not help but stop for a moment to play with the child.

Don Bartolo's little boy had gotten quite well, with the help of the medicines which Don Sebastián's small loan had paid for. Now he sat happily in the lap of his seven-year-old sister, who was playing patty-cake with him. As she clapped his little brown hands together she sang

Tortillitas pa' mamá!
Tortillitas pa' papá!

She sang *"pa"* instead of *"para"* to fit the rhythm. The verse means, "Little *tortillas* for mama! Little *tortillas* for papa!"

When Luis squatted on one heel in front of him, the baby reached out and took two handfuls

of Luis's shining, wet, black hair. Luis laughed. When the baby started trying to poke fingers into his eyes, he took him from his sister and held him on his knee while he talked nonsense.

The baby's crowing brought the child's mother to the door. She was a solidly built woman who never lost the smile in her eyes no matter how hard her life became.

"The children all love you, Luis," she said. "It's too bad you haven't a baby brother of your own. Where are you going, with fresh clothes on and your hair combed?"

Luis handed the baby to his mother and smoothed his mussed hair. "To the home of Señora Castelar," he said, holding out the green sweater which he carried over his arm. "Her daughter Raquel has promised to mend this for me."

Luis had been in the home of the Castelar women not over five minutes when he decided that we must build this place into our model. They had only two rooms and a small patio where they did their cooking. But everything was so clean and pretty that it charmed Luis. They had saved some nice furniture from a better time when Raquel's father was alive. The lace pieces on the tables and chairs were lovely in Luis's eyes; so was the embroidered bedspread he could see when Raquel went into the other room for her knitting things. Raquel and her mother had made the lace and embroidery themselves.

The thing that mattered more than furniture and lace was the feeling that these two women had given to their small rooms. They had made this a place where people could live pleasantly together and enjoy one another, a place where one wanted to be. It had the feeling of home.

Raquel sat down in an easy chair to knit. Her mother had gone out into the patio to get supper. As I told you, we eat late in Guadalajara.

"You will have supper with us, of course," Raquel said, and when Luis tried to say that he was not hungry, she smiled in a way that showed him he could not make her believe such a fib. She began their talk by asking about the model, which Luis was naturally pleased to tell about. That led to telling about his home in the *vecindad* and his trips with his father.

Telling me about it afterward, Luis said that he did not know exactly how it came about. But

132

by the time supper was on the table, he felt as if he belonged in Raquel's home. He felt happy. And he felt as if nothing bad could ever happen to him so long as he was there.

Raquel, he found, was as much girl as woman. She loved fun, and after supper she and Luis began telling stories of things that had happened to them. Luis told the one he had told us about pulling the burro out of the mud, and another about riding a calf on his uncle's little ranch. He got up and acted the stories out. Even Señora

Castelar laughed until the tears stood in her fine, brown eyes.

Raquel told about a silly young woman coming with her very much embarrassed young husband

to buy clothes for a trip. She played all the parts—
the haughty young bride, the mild little husband, herself, and the store manager—turning
herself into each one when the time came. It was
very gay. They laughed themselves out of breath.
When Raquel had finished, she and Luis sat,
comfortable and quiet for a time, while Raquel's
mother went out to make some chocolate.

There came a sudden knocking on the door—
loud, as if a heavy fist were striking. Raquel gave
the door a puzzled look, as much as to say, "Who
in the world could that be?" and went to open it.

There stood Luis's father, looking dignified and
very angry. "I have come for my son," he said.

"Do come in, Don Sebastián," said Raquel.
"My mother and I have been enjoying Luis very
much. He is such a nice boy—and amusing
besides!"

Don Sebastián did not want to come in, but
he did. He stood looking down at Luis as if he
were a strayed burro. He kept turning his hat
in his hand and Luis knew he was nervous. Perhaps Raquel and her mother made him uneasy.
He did not have much to do with women in his
business. He was not used to them.

"Come on," he said to Luis. "We're leaving in the morning at four o'clock. It's time you were in bed."

"Do sit down, Don Sebastián," said Raquel. "My mother's feelings will be hurt if you leave without tasting her chocolate."

It was very funny to Luis. His father did not want to sit down. He wanted to pull Luis out of there fast. But he sat down anyway, on the edge of a comfortable chair. Don Sebastián can handle burros and men, but he did not know what to do about Raquel. She picked up Luis's green sweater and began to knit, looking sidewise at Don Sebastián from under her eyelashes.

Don Sebastián looked angrier than before. He took a deep breath to say something, let the breath go, drew another—and ended by saying nothing. Raquel all of a sudden put the knitting in her lap and looked at Don Sebastián in a very humble way, as if she were afraid she had done something wrong. "Is it that you do not wish me to mend the hole in your son's sweater, Don Sebastián?"

"I can take care of my boy!" said Luis's father in a stiff voice. "I can buy him all the clothes he needs."

"Of course, Don Sebastián! Whoever would doubt that you do very well by Luis? But the godmother who takes care of your son—she is a very old woman, indeed. She can no longer do the things that a boy needs done for him. You are a good father, but you cannot do everything for Luis that a woman can do." Raquel smiled suddenly. "Or can you, Don Sebastián?"

Luis's father looked almost startled. "No, no, and no!" he said. "I—I am not anything of a woman."

Raquel's mother then came in with chocolate all frothy in the cup and smelling most wonderful. There were little cakes and a little napkin with a lace border.

Don Sebastián picked the napkin up in his big fingers as if it were a butterfly wing. He balanced the plate on his knee and took a sip of the chocolate.

A look of surprise came into Don Sebastián's face. "But this is very good, *señora*. I have not tasted such chocolate since——"

He did not finish. But the way he was looking at his son made Luis understand that he had meant to say, "Since my boy's mother died."

Raquel's mother thanked him in a quiet voice, and Raquel went on, holding up Luis's sweater.

"Consider this sweater," she said. "It is much too good to throw away. But if it is not mended, then you might as well throw it away. And the godmother is much too old to mend it."

"She doesn't even know how to knit!" Luis said.

Don Sebastián is very honest, but also very stubborn. "It is true that she could not have mended the sweater," he said. "But I can take care of my son! We do not need favors from anyone!"

"That is an unkind thought!" said Raquel's mother. "Do you think we would do this small thing to shame you, *señor?* We are only thinking of the boy's happiness, like yourself!"

Raquel said, smiling, "We are not the ones who are doing the favor, anyhow. It is you, *señor,* who are doing us a favor. We take so much pleasure in having Luis with us. He has such good manners——"

She said many things so nice that Luis blushed and lowered his head.

Don Sebastián was pleased to hear her speak well of his son. The look on his face grew softer, and he sat back quite happily in his chair to finish the chocolate. Raquel asked him where he and Luis were going on their trip, and before Luis could think of a way to stop him, he was talking about—eggs.

It embarrassed Luis to have his father talk about eggs to so pretty a woman. But it was better to have him talk about eggs than get up and leave. Luis felt unhappy when Don Sebastián finished his chocolate and it was time to go.

Raquel had handed Luis his sweater some time before, but without saying anything. He put it on, and thanked her very much. His father thanked her also, but grumpily.

138

Raquel did not seem to notice. She stood in the doorway and put her hand on Luis's shoulder.

"Come back, Luis," she said. "It makes me happy to have you. I have wanted a brother to do things for, ever since God took my own brother from us when he was a tiny boy. Come back to me when you have finished your trip."

Then she turned to Don Sebastián, speaking severely. "As for you, Señor Sebastián Cota, I expect you back also. I wish you to bring me an egg!"

Don Sebastián does not like being told what to do by anyone, man or woman. Luis heard his teeth snap together, where he stood in the shadow. Then the joke of it, the silliness of carrying an egg in his hand to Raquel, one single egg out of all the dozens he and Luis would buy—the joke struck him. He laughed and laughed like a breeze shaking a tree.

When he got his breath, he said, "Truly, *señorita*, I will bring you an egg! The sweetest egg in all the great State of Jalisco."

On summer nights in Guadalajara the air touches your cheek like a young mother running her fingers lightly over the hair of a child. Our city stands too high to be really hot but not high enough to be cold. We have rivers and rain, so the air does not have the ovenlike dryness of the north of Mexico. But there is not enough ground water or downpour to make the air sticky. Guadalajara has a just-right climate—or so it seems to us.

Others were enjoying this night. Luis and his father passed a group of young men lounging against a wall at a corner. A guitar hummed and cried, and some of the men sang. Across the street another young man stood at a window, "playing the bear." Behind the window bars sat a girl in a dark dress with water birds printed in white on the cloth. When she moved, the birds seemed to flutter as if trying to escape through the bars.

These sights and sounds pressed themselves into Luis's mind. He was working himself up to a very bold act. At times like these, when a person is doing something that makes him feel strongly, everything he sees or hears becomes important and clear. You know how this is.

I do not know why it is called "playing the bear" when a young man stands on the sidewalk and talks to a girl through a window. It is a Spanish custom. Young men play the bear in Guadalajara for the same reason we dance the old dances along with modern ones. The young men do not need to stand outside. Nowadays the girls can invite them inside when they like. The girls can go out with their boy friends just about the same as in the United States. But it is fun to play the bear and so the young men do it on soft, pleasant evenings in the old *barrios* where the houses are built Spanish style and the people have a fondness for old ways.

"I'm not going with you!" Luis said to his father.

Don Sebastián turned from watching the young man at the girl's window. "What's that?"

"I said I'm not going after eggs with you. I'm going to get a job here."

Even in the shadows, Luis could see his father grow angry. His temper showed in the set of his shoulders and the way his hands swung as he turned. Yet Luis felt safe. He had known his father to be so angry with burros that he could not speak. But Don Sebastián had never beaten a burro.

"What job could you get?" he asked, in a quiet, furious voice.

"A rich man named Señor Pidal told me to come to him. He will give me a good job and pay me a man's wages."

"I have heard people speak of Señor Pidal," Don Sebastián said. "He is new in the city. But they say he will do big things. Is it true that he will give you a job?"

"It is true," Luis answered. "He gave me his card and told me to come to him."

The anger had gone suddenly from Don Sebastián. He looked smaller. His shoulders had a discouraged droop.

"Son," he said, laying a hand on Luis's shoulder, "I have not had much to give you—hard work, little money, no home at all. If you can do better for yourself—go to Señor Pidal, and go with God!"

Don Sebastián turned on his heel and walked with long, quick steps into the darkness. Though Luis felt suddenly sad and rather ashamed, he did not try to catch up. He knew that his father would not want him to.

CHAPTER 12

A *Star* of Chiles

It is early morning. Luis is walking across the pavement with the man who sells *chiles* in the market and lives in the same *vecindad* as Luis. The man is bent in the back and the knees and the fingers. His mind is bent also, so he does nothing but complain about how hard the times are and how little he makes.

144

He goes grumbling to a big truck that has drawn up beside the market. This one is full of *chiles*—big green ones, little green ones, middle-sized red ones, and tiny red ones. It is wonderful what a good Mexican cook can do with *chiles*. Most people in the United States think we use them to make a burning inside the mouth. But in Guadalajara we use the strength of the *chile* wisely—as one uses salt. Since there are many kinds of *chiles*, we can use them to give to each dish the exact flavor we wish.

Here, then, is Luis, walking with the old *chile*-seller to the truck which has just come in from the market gardens beside Lake Chapala. Chapala is a very big lake of a misty-blue color, 32 miles from our city. We get most of our vegetables from the rich lands along the edges. From the lake itself, fishermen in canoes take small white fish which are very good to eat.

The truck has already stopped at the office of the man who buys and sells vegetables *por mayor*—that is, "in large" (a wholesaler, you would say in the United States). This large seller has given the driver an order to come to our market and deliver to each little seller of *chiles* as many as he needs. The man with Luis buys very small amounts, for he has little trade and less money. He is sunk so deep in his own troubles that even the golden light of a Guadalajara morning cannot drive away the darkness of his mind.

It is not so with the men working nearby.

In front of the market two red trucks are unloading ears of corn. Two great mounds of green ears are growing on the paving stones between the market and the street. The men are strong; their T shirts cling to them as they work and you can see their muscles ripple and bulge. Across their faces go small smiles like flickers of warm firelight. They work busily and silently, thinking of good times to come, pleased with the growing heaps of corn.

Beyond the corn, at the side of the market, jokes are flying through the quiet air. A man stands on some crates piled high in a truck. The crates are made of sticks, and between the sticks poke the heads of chickens and ducks. The man hands the crates down to two others standing on the ground and there is plenty of squawking. The man on the truck looks down and recognizes Luis. "I saw your father up the road, young one! Why aren't you with him?"

"I'm having my vacation," answers Luis, grinning up at him.

"Vacation," says the man with a snort. "That's a good joke! Workmen who belong to the big unions get vacations. Government workers get vacations. Bankers and school children get vacations. But burro drivers! The road is a year long for them, and every day begins before sunup. I think your father left you behind because you are too lazy to be any help."

"I wouldn't talk," answers Luis. "The only reason you are working now is because your brother-in-law got tired of feeding you free."

There is a big shout of laughter, and the man on the truck shakes his fist at Luis—though in fun. Luis says, taking the smile from his face, "No fooling, I am sick of the egg business —and burros, too! I am going to ask Don Agustín Mendosa to give me a job."

The man on the truck laughs and says, "Don Agustín Mendosa is a fine gentleman. He doesn't need any lazy boys with sharp tongues."

While Luis is thinking of an answer, an old, trembling voice comes to them from beyond the truck. It is the voice of an old man who squats all day in the shade of a green tree near the side door of the market. Around him his turkeys, each tied with a cord from one foot to a peg in the ground, peck restlessly at the grass growing in the cracks between the flagstones.

"I wouldn't be too sure that Don Agustín won't give him a job!" says the old man. "Luis goes in and out of his house like one of the family."

"Luis," he asked, "is it true that you and the Mendosa boy are making a model of Guadalajara?"

Luis says it is true. All work stops for a little while because everyone wants to know about the model. The men begin to look at Luis in a new way and to speak to him more respectfully. This is because he is a friend of my father. In talking with these men, Luis finds out that they think my father is a good man who is always fair with everybody. Also, they think that he has done a great deal for Guadalajara by working on important committees, like the one that runs the hospital for mothers and babies.

"I don't see why we don't get more men like Don Agustín in the government," one of the men says. "He is rich and of a very fine family—but he understands the people, too. He is always thinking of what we need."

Luis does not answer this, because the old *chile*-seller calls and asks if he is really going to help him carry the *chiles* inside, or has he just been fooling? Luis goes to help him, and they carry the *chiles* into the dimness of the market.

The old man begins arranging his *chiles* in careless little heaps on a low table scarcely wider than a bench. He sits behind this table with a box of *chiles* beside him so that he can put out more

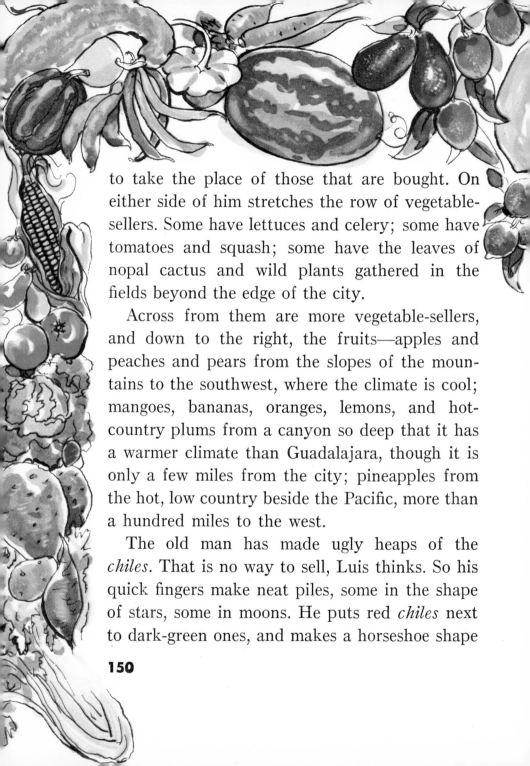

to take the place of those that are bought. On either side of him stretches the row of vegetable-sellers. Some have lettuces and celery; some have tomatoes and squash; some have the leaves of nopal cactus and wild plants gathered in the fields beyond the edge of the city.

Across from them are more vegetable-sellers, and down to the right, the fruits—apples and peaches and pears from the slopes of the mountains to the southwest, where the climate is cool; mangoes, bananas, oranges, lemons, and hot-country plums from a canyon so deep that it has a warmer climate than Guadalajara, though it is only a few miles from the city; pineapples from the hot, low country beside the Pacific, more than a hundred miles to the west.

The old man has made ugly heaps of the *chiles*. That is no way to sell, Luis thinks. So his quick fingers make neat piles, some in the shape of stars, some in moons. He puts red *chiles* next to dark-green ones, and makes a horseshoe shape

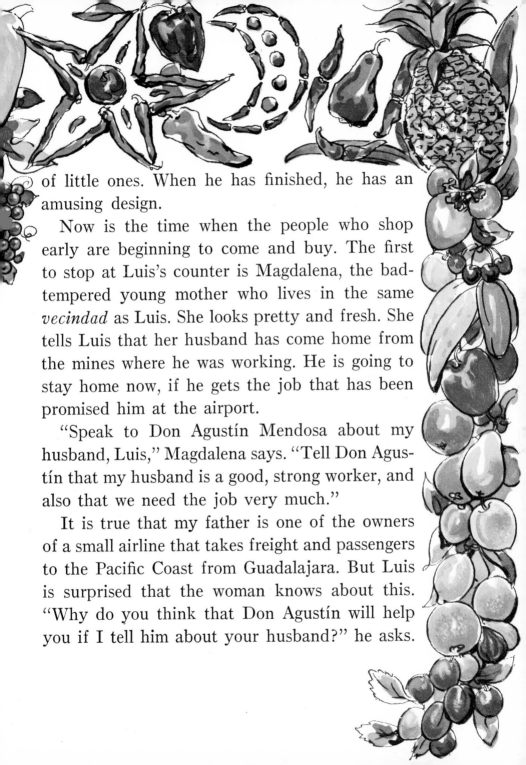

of little ones. When he has finished, he has an amusing design.

Now is the time when the people who shop early are beginning to come and buy. The first to stop at Luis's counter is Magdalena, the bad-tempered young mother who lives in the same *vecindad* as Luis. She looks pretty and fresh. She tells Luis that her husband has come home from the mines where he was working. He is going to stay home now, if he gets the job that has been promised him at the airport.

"Speak to Don Agustín Mendosa about my husband, Luis," Magdalena says. "Tell Don Agustín that my husband is a good, strong worker, and also that we need the job very much."

It is true that my father is one of the owners of a small airline that takes freight and passengers to the Pacific Coast from Guadalajara. But Luis is surprised that the woman knows about this. "Why do you think that Don Agustín will help you if I tell him about your husband?" he asks.

"Everyone knows that Don Agustín has a heart. He is not one of those who thinks of men simply as makers of money for him. He looks out at the suffering of this world, and wherever he can help, he helps."

When Magdalena has gone, the woman at the next table looks at Luis curiously. She is a calm, dark-skinned woman in a dress so clean one notices it. She sits behind carrots and peas, all very neatly arranged. She says, "Magdalena gets lonesome and restless when her husband is away. So she goes out more than she ought to. My mother used to say to me, 'Daughter, you will be tempted to leave the home. But remember that *casada* means what it says—*casada!*'"

I will have to give you the English so that you will know why Luis laughed. *Casa* in our language means house. Our word for "married" is "housed" (*casada*). The market woman's mother had told her to remember that after a girl is married she is supposed to stay in her own house and not run around.

Luis grins at the woman. "You speak the truth, *señora*. But you are quite a long way from home yourself, aren't you?"

The market woman laughs, "You are too smart for your size!" she says. "I will tell you a secret that all we city women know in our hearts. It is better to work hard, to get up early and stay up late to care for one's family and go to a job during the day, than it is to stay home all the time. Look and listen!"

The market has begun to fill up, and voices are rising all through it. They sound like the gentle buzzing of early-morning bees coming into a hayfield. At many of the fruit and vegetable stands people have stopped, by ones and twos and threes. They stand at ease, trading news and jokes and thoughts.

"I love it," the market woman says, stretching her arms as if to take in all of the old market. "If I did not work I would be unhappy and bored. To fill the empty days I would take four times as long as need be to do the household tasks. I would have too much time alone in which to envy my neighbors. In the country villages, the life of a woman in the home is often very good. A wife has her family and her god-relations. In the city most households live apart, among strangers. We city women are happier when we have some work—

unless, of course, one is rich. Life must be very fine for the wife of Don Agustín Mendosa."

"Why, *señora?*" asks Luis.

"Why?" says the market woman in surprise. "Because she has a fine house and automobiles and lovely clothes——"

The woman stops with a thoughtful look on her face. "No," she says, "I see many women come into the market. Some are as rich as the Señora Mendosa, but few seem as happy. It must be that her husband is as good as people say. Is it not true that Don Agustín is kind and generous?"

"Yes," says Luis, and stops because two women are coming toward his stall.

One is rather heavy-faced and plainly dressed. It is clear to Luis that she is a servant. The other is a young girl all in black. Her clothes are of the finest cloth; the scarf draped over her head is light as a black cobweb. She is a slender girl who carries her head very high and with great pride. Her face is very white, which makes her mouth seem red as rose petals and her large black eyes very bright. She is very pretty and looks as if she knows it. But at the moment she seems to be walking in an unhappy dream.

154

As she comes nearer, she keeps looking at the little piles of *chiles* Luis has made on the table. The servant wishes to pass by, but the girl walks over to the table where Luis sits. She stops before a pile of *chiles* laid out in the shape of a star. Luis has put little red *chiles* at the points of the green star, like little tips of flame. The girl puts out slender white fingers and touches the *chiles* lightly. Her nails are the same color as her lips.

The old *chile*-seller is staring at her with his mouth open. He is so surprised to have her stop at his table that he cannot speak. But Luis is no more tongue-tied than usual.

"The finest *chiles* in the State of Jalisco, *señorita,*" he says. "They are so fresh that last night's dew is still on them, and so delicate—*señorita,* only yourself can understand the flavor of these *chiles*. They were grown for a princess, *señorita— una princesa como usted* (—a princess like yourself)!"

The girl's eyes and mouth flash Luis a smile like sunlight flashing on the little silver waves of Lake Chapala.

"You are as bold as a little brass bull," she says. "I suppose your *chiles* are no worse than

others. Buy some, María." The servant buys so many that the old *chile*-seller is made very happy. But the girl seems to go back into her unhappy dream as she walks slowly away. The market woman in the next stand leans over to whisper, "That is the *novia* (sweetheart) of Don Arturo Amador."

"*No me diga!* (You don't say!)" says Luis, very interested. The woman nods firmly.

156

"It is the truth. They are saying around the
market that she quarreled with Don Arturo and
that he went away. This could be a reason why she
looks so sad these days. It is strange to see her
look unhappy. She's a gay young thing."

"Does she come often to the market?" asks
Luis.

"Quite often. Her father is very strict and old
fashioned. He never lets her go out unless some
person in her family is along, or a servant he
trusts. He makes her come to the market because
he thinks it is the duty of every girl to learn to
run her own house. He is right about that! But
he runs her life for her too much. In this time
we live in, a woman has to learn to think for
herself."

CHAPTER 13

How Pidal Took in Luis

Luis walked back and forth several times in front of Señor Pidal's house, looking it over. He did not know just how to get in. The house looked to Luis like blocks set one on top of the other by a child too young to build carefully. This house was in the style called modern. You have many such houses in the United States, and we have quite a few in Mexico. But it

158

is only in the newer, richer neighborhoods, out toward the edges of the cities, that one finds them.

These new neighborhoods, like the one where Señor Pidal lived, are called *colonias*. Instead of being like little towns within the city, as the old *barrios* are, the *colonias* are like your neighborhoods of homes in the United States, like the parts of your cities which I have heard called residential districts. The people in the *colonias* do not have the feeling that they belong to one big family, as do the people in the *barrios*. Their houses are like yours in the United States, each standing separate from the others. In the *colonias* there are many, many different styles of houses. Most of them stand in the midst of gardens, instead of having the garden inside as we do in the old *barrios*. I mean they have yards instead of patios.

I am telling you all this so you will know what the parts of our model which have *colonia* written on them are like. We did not build these parts, but only marked them out with chalk. Some *colonias* are pretty, but there is nothing special about them.

Luis felt lonely as he walked up and down in front of Señor Pidal's house. To be in this rich man's *colonia* was to him like being in a strange city. And there was something strange about the house itself. It seemed like a bank or factory, a place where people could stay, but surely not a home where a family could live and love.

At last he decided to go around by the walk that led to the back. Here he found a door onto a porch, and from this door came a woman's very pretty voice singing in the Italian language.

The song was more beautiful than the singer. She answered Luis's knock by coming to the screen door and telling him to go away. She spoke roughly, in poor Spanish. Two of her front teeth were missing, and her nose was the shape of a light bulb. Luis smiled pleasantly at her, held up the card Pidal had given him, and asked if the *señor* was at home.

The woman took the card and went away muttering. When she came back she opened the door and watched him come in with a close look that made him notice her eyes. They were beautiful eyes, behind very long, soft lashes. They were eyes that remembered sad and terrible things.

160

"Come in," she said, and as she led Luis through the kitchen she went on muttering to herself. "Yes indeed, come in, little fly. Come in! You will find the spider most polite. Oh, most polite!"

Luis was used to hearing his old godmother mutter to herself. He had gotten in the way of hearing her without really paying attention. He listened to this woman in the same way. She seemed to be Señor Pidal's cook, for on the way through the kitchen she stopped to stir something red in a pot on the stove. It smelled very good and rather strange.

The cook pushed open the swinging door into the dining room and let Luis go in by himself. Señor Pidal was sitting at a long table of some dark, shining wood. It was a dining table, but he was writing, not eating. Pidal held out his hand to Luis, though he did not get up.

"My young friend the charcoal-seller!" he said, smiling. "How kind of you to come!"

Naturally, it made Luis feel very good to be talked to so politely. Señor Pidal had that way I have told you about—a way of making it seem that he was doing a favor when he spoke to you at all. And to have Pidal seem glad that he had come made Luis so proud and pleased that, for once, he could not say anything.

Señor Pidal did not seem to mind that Luis was tongue-tied. He ran his hand over the front part of his head, where the hair had gone, leaving smooth brown skin. With his other hand, he fished in his pocket. All this while he was looking Luis over with eyes as cool and shiny as wet, brown stones. The baldness did not make him look foolish or ugly. It simply made him seem old enough to be important. The room had heavy hangings of red velvet beside the tall windows. The dining chairs standing around the wall had high, carved backs. They were the kind of chairs that kings and dukes sat in, in the pictures Luis had seen.

"You have come because you wish to be one of my men, have you not?" said Señor Pidal.

"Yes, sir," said Luis. "I would like very much to work for you."

From the pocket of his red silk robe, Señor Pidal took a silver cigarette case. The robe looked very expensive. In it Pidal made Luis think of the men who ruled Mexico in the old times, when the Mexicans were not free. Luis listened his hardest, trying to understand everything so that he could do all this man asked in a way that pleased him.

"I have important work for you," Pidal said. "It is work that I would not trust to everybody. The person I need must be brave. He must be more than brave. He must dare to take chances no one else would think of. He must be honest and loyal to me. And he must keep his mouth shut like a small jail from which nothing escapes. Do you think you are such a person, Luis?"

If it had been possible for Luis to feel any better than he already did, he would have been lifted up because Señor Pidal remembered his name. But Luis could stand no more of such high, serious feelings. The imp came out in him

and he said, "My father calls me a burro, Señor Pidal. But I could be a tiger if I had the chance. Try me and you will see that I have a striped skin and sharp claws."

Señor Pidal did not laugh in answer to Luis's grin. His eyes grew narrow as he looked closely to see whether Luis was making fun of him. He saw that Luis was simply full of good spirits.

"I am not fond of wild animals," Pidal said, "or foolish boys! But I might have use for a foolish boy who has worked with animals. Have there been bulls in your life?"

Luis had been frightened by Pidal's look and his hard tone of voice. But these words made his eyes dance again. Every Mexican boy plays at being a bullfighter, even though he has to put horns on a large dog and pretend that it is a fierce bull. Up and down the roads on travels with his father, Luis had bothered many bulls until they charged him. Pidal's question set his brain buzzing with excitement and wondering. He could only nod in answer.

Pidal's eyes told no more than his mouth, which he kept closed. The man sat for a time making up his mind whether the boy should do some special thing—or not do it.

164

At last Pidal reached out with a swift, smooth
motion. He took a pen from a marble holder and
wrote several lines. He put the paper into an envelope and wrote an address. He held out the note
and spoke slowly and very clearly, driving each
word into Luis's mind.

"Deliver this message. Do what you are told.
When you return to Guadalajara, come straight
to me."

Pidal's look made Luis feel as if he had swallowed something cold and strange. *"Si senor,"* he
whispered, and hurried out of the house.

CHAPTER 14

Luis and the Flying Bulls

Less than an hour later Luis sat on the hard, dirty floor of an airplane feeling as if he were in a dream, though wide awake. All around him the noise of the motors roared, shaking the floor, shaking Luis. Beside him lay a man who had his clothes pulled away from his middle. A rubber bag full of ice lay on his body. Beads of sweat stood on his forehead, for he was in great pain. Behind Luis the inside of the plane stretched away like a shadowy tunnel. There were no seats—only five huge boxes standing on the floor.

The motor deafened Luis with a rising roar, and the big machine seemed to stand on tiptoe. Then it was running forward, faster, faster—and faster.

Luis caught hold of a piece of metal on the wall and pulled himself to his feet so that he could look out a window. Below him was a clump of trees, and beyond it the red roof of a house. A child waved at the plane, and it came to Luis that he was flying, high above the earth. He clung to the window frame shuddering from head to foot.

The roofs of Guadalajara had dropped from sight when Luis felt a hand like a steel hook grip his ankle and pull. He staggered, and dropped to his knees beside the sick man. The man cursed him in a whisper, calling him "coward," and "little girl," and "stupid rabbit." Luis became more ashamed than afraid. By the time the man had stopped cursing, he had stopped shaking.

"Take this sugar," the man said, touching a box beside him. "Feed it to the bulls. Talk to them. They are children and need to be soothed. If you love your life, talk to them sweetly. If they keep on stamping and throwing themselves around the way they are doing now, they will unbalance the airplane and we will crash!"

Luis took the box and made his way back to the big boxes. The plane lurched and he staggered. And as he went he heard above the motors' roar, the low, frightened bawling of bulls and the scrape of horns on wood, and the crash of their bodies as they threshed and fought to get free.

The boxes were higher than Luis's head, about three feet wide, and eight feet long. He found small, square openings in the ends of the boxes. The sugar was in big, brown cakes. Luis broke off pieces and poked them into the openings. Wet, rough tongues licked the sugar from his hands, and he talked to the bulls each in turn, calling them pet names.

This struck him as an odd thing to do—after the bulls had grown quiet and he had time to sit with his back against the wall and think. These bulls were being flown to a town near the border between Mexico and the United States. Tomorrow they would be killed. Luis had heard the pilot say that they had to be on hand for a bullfight the next day. This was the reason why the airplane went on, instead of waiting in Guadalajara until someone could come from a ranch and take the sick man's place. Tomorrow the bulls would be killed with swords, and Luis had been feeding them sugar and calling them pet names! The sick man was strange, too. He had insisted on staying with the bulls, not trusting Luis to keep them quiet and content. The bulls were his children, he said. Now the man was asleep. The doctor had given him a pill.

It was the doctor to whom Luis had delivered Pidal's note. The doctor had acted strangely, too. Seated at his desk in a room lined with big books, he read the note, tore it into little pieces, and looked up at Luis with eyes that were too unhappy for his young, good-looking face.

"How did you get into this?" he asked. "You're too young to have a rope round your neck like the rest of us." Then, seeing Luis's puzzled look, the doctor shook his head. "Never mind," he said. "Let's go. But I'll give you one piece of advice. Don't ask questions. The less you know, the better it will be for you."

They had driven to the airport, where the plane stood waiting at the edge of the field. The doctor tended to the sick man and gave Luis a pill. The pilot fastened the door, and the engines began to roar.

To understand all that he had seen and heard was like trying to read a letter that has been torn into little bits. Luis could not make sense of any part of this adventure. So he went and fed more sugar to the bulls. Afterward, he looked out the window. It had grown dark, and all he saw were stars that looked very cold and far away.

Hour after hour the plane droned through the sky like a night-flying bee. Luis, being half numb with cold and weariness, scarcely knew when it began to circle for a landing. But the bulls knew. Luis had all he could do to keep them from going wild during the time they were dropping from the sky.

Men came into the plane, and carried out the sick man. An ambulance clanged up and took him away. By that time the men had lifted down the first of the bulls, still in his box. A tall person with black mustaches gave orders in a booming voice.

Everyone seemed to like him. A few of the men called him Señor Topete, but most of them called him Don Tomás. Luis guessed he must be the well-known owner of the Ranch of The Three Rivers, near Guadalajara, and also owner of the bulls.

The men put the bulls on a low trailer nearly as long as the airplane, and trundled them off into the darkness No one had spoken to Luis since the plane landed. The night had a faint smell of dust and dry country plants—far different from the warm, sweet-smelling nights of Guadalajara. The feeling of being far, far from home crept over him.

"Luis!"

The sound of his own name made him jump. Don Tomás was motioning him to get into a car that stood near the plane. The big *ranchero* kept silence as he sent the car down a steep road that twisted among hills. But even his silence seemed friendly. When the car rounded a sharp bend and Luis saw the sky lit with a great golden glow, he was not afraid to speak.

"What's that?" Luis asked, pressing his nose to the window. "What makes the sky so bright?"

"Thousands of lights, perhaps millions," Don Tomás said in his deep voice. "They are in the city of San Diego, fifteen miles north of here, in the United States."

"When can I go there?" Luis whispered, still staring out the window. "Can I go tomorrow?"

"It is not allowed, unless you have a paper giving special permission. This you could not get. Besides, you work for Señor Pidal, remember."

They passed through the streets of Tijuana and went through a gate in the fence around the arena where the bullfights are held. Luis helped get the bulls out of the boxes and into a corral. But he remembered very little about all this. His excitement had gone, leaving a tired, mixed-up feeling. He was thankful when Don Tomás took him to a pile of coverings that looked like quilts and smelled of horse.

He woke to the sound of hoofs beating softly on dirt. A horse came galloping toward him between tall posts that held up the seats of the arena which had the shape of a dunce-cap stood on end.

A blindfold was tied over the horse's eyes. The rider carried a spear in his hand. His feet were poked into square iron boxes instead of regular stirrups. Luis understood that the rider was trying out this horse to see whether he could be managed in the arena, where the bulls would charge him again and again. He sat up and had his first close look at the soft things he had been sleeping on. They were made like quilts, and bright-colored like quilts. But by their odd shapes he knew them to be padded armour to keep horses from being torn to pieces by the bulls' horns.

Above Luis's head the outward-sloping curve of the arena was bright with sun. More horses stood in a corral nearby. On the corral fence men and boys sat like roosting birds. They were watching a young fellow spin a rope with lazy, graceful motions. Other men stood talking in little groups, and some were walking here and there This good natured bustling was just like home in Guadalajara. Luis jumped up, grinning, and went to join Don Tomás Topete, who had stopped to watch the cowboy spin his rope.

I have already told you how hard it is to keep from smiling back at Luis when he grins. Smile wrinkles came into Don Tomás's big brown face.

"A very good morning to you, son," he said. "Your sleep did you good."

He asked Luis the name of his father, and other friendly questions. But Luis could see that he

listened to the answers with only one ear. Don
Tomás tugged at his mustache, and glanced at
every man who passed. For a big, strong man who
lived on a ranch, Don Tomás was very nervous.
After a little, he asked Luis how long he had
worked for Pidal.

"It is not yet one day."

Into Don Tomás's eyes came a sad look that reminded Luis of the doctor who had taken him to
the airport in Guadalajara. "The very first day!"
he said. "And he has sent you on a trip like this."

Luis thought that Don Tomás meant he was not
old enough or wise enough to care for the bulls.

174

"I have worked with animals all my life, *señor*. Truly, I took good care of the bulls."

"The bulls are wild as tigers, but they are in good shape," said a cheerful voice behind Luis. "Whoever sent this young man made a good choice."

Luis had spun around at the first word. The speaker was a small man with pink cheeks and snapping eyes. He rocked back on his heels and puffed on a big cigar. He was feeling very, very good.

Luis did not wish to take too much credit to himself. He said, "The man from the ranch was

175

sick. Señor Pidal sent me because he could not find anyone else in a hurry."

"Pidal?" said the small man in a questioning tone. "Pidal?"

"He means Pindray," Don Tomás said quickly. "Pancho Pindray. One of my men in Guadalajara."

"Pidal or Pindray," the small man said cheerfully, "he sent a good boy." He clamped his cigar between his teeth and reached into his pocket for some papers. "Look, Don Tomás, everything is fixed up! The money will be paid to you the minute the bank opens in the morning."

They went on talking business, seeming to forget Luis, who kept his ears open. The small man was named Lerdo. He was buying the bulls from Don Tomás Topete. With his two partners he was putting on a whole series of bullfights in Tijuana.

When they had finished their talk, the two men shook hands, as we Mexicans do when we leave someone we have been talking to—even though we expect to see him again in a little while. Señor Lerdo shook Luis's hand, too, then walked rapidly away puffing cigar smoke.

Don Tomás took Luis by the arm and leaned down so that he could speak to him in a low voice.

"Never say Pidal's name unless you are talking to someone who is working for him. He would be very angry if he knew you had spoken of him to Lerdo. And when Pidal is angry——"

"Please don't tell him, Don Tomás," Luis begged.

Don Tomás had spoken as if Pidal might do something terrible to Luis. To Luis this meant that Pidal might not let him go on being one of his men. Just then, he could not imagine anything more terrible. But this was not what Don Tomás had in mind at all. Pidal was one of the most cruel men he had ever known.

Don Tomás's face grew even more sad and worried than before. He thought of giving Luis some money and telling him to lose himself in Tijuana.

But Luis would not be able to find work in this small city where people from all parts of Mexico come by thousands to wait for a chance to cross into the United States. If Luis went back to Guadalajara knowing what kind of man Pidal was, he might try to run away. If he did this, Pidal would tell the police that Luis had run off with some of his money. The very worst thing would be for Luis to know the truth about the bulls he had helped to bring. They were stolen bulls. Luis was not the kind of boy to be trusted with so shameful a secret. If Pidal even guessed that Luis knew the truth—Luis's life would not be safe.

Don Tomás could not decide what to do. So he put Luis's problem off, which was his way with hard problems.

"Keep your mouth shut!" he said gruffly, and walked off.

Don Tomás's back was not interesting to look at. Luis turned, and saw a small, serious man tearing a cigarette open. Several others were gathered close about him, all watching closely. The man threw away the tobacco and tore the cigarette paper into strips. He wrote on each of these, then crumpled them into tight little wads. There were three. He put them into a hat. Someone laid another hat, with its crown up, on top of the first. Then one of the men standing close by put his hand in between the hats and drew out one of the slips. Two others did the same.

These three were the men sent by the *matadores* (bull-killers) to take care of their business. The slips were drawn from the hat to decide which *matador* was to fight first, which second, and which last. When the drawing was over, the men went to look at the bulls.

Luis followed them down a very narrow passageway. There were small openings in the wall. In front of each opening was a high, wooden shield like a small piece of fence standing out two feet or so from the wall. The feeding troughs for the bulls lay along the wall close beside these openings. If a bull charged a man who was putting hay into a trough, the man could duck back behind the shield.

The men crowded into a couple of these openings to look over the bulls. Luis climbed the wall and looked over. The bulls were all black. They looked as if they had no fat on them at all— only muscle. Their sweeping horns were like rounded swords.

The men quickly decided that it would be all right to take the bulls into the ring to show off their tricks. The *matadores* needed to know what they would have to watch out for, or the bulls might kill them. Luis trooped back with the others along the narrow passage and climbed the stairs to a platform built along a runway leading to the ring. A number of ropes led to doors opening into this runway; the two longest ropes opened and shut the gate of the *corral* where the bulls stood tossing their horns. Several men crouched down on the platform and took the ropes in their hands.

Some other men, who were out of sight, began yelling and throwing stones at the bulls. The black beasts crowded forward in a tight group.

Then two of them turned and looked as if they meant to charge the yelling men. These men were standing safe in the entrances to the *corral*. They yelled and threw more stones. Very slowly, turning often to glare at the men, the bulls moved toward the gate.

Don Tomás Topete took a place beside Luis, and a moment later two other men came up and stood behind them. They were all four standing behind the men who held the ropes, out of the way. Luis was too much interested in the herding of the bulls to pay the others much attention. The bulls were stamping and snorting and trying to kill the men who now and then ran into the *corral* to yell and wave their arms. It was very exciting. Luis was startled to hear a voice behind him say, "Look at that big one by the gate! Somebody has changed the brand on him as sure as my name is Pedro Palma."

The brand mark on the bull's side was a scar made by a hot iron. Each rancher makes his own mark in this way, as your ranchers do in the United States. This brand was a very fancy one, made up of three letters. It was Don Tomás's brand; these bulls had come from his ranch. Since Luis had liked Don Tomás from the start, it made him angry to hear the man say that the brand had been changed. Cattle thieves changed brands to make it seem that the animals were their own. Don Tomás was angry too. He turned and said in his big, booming voice, "Be careful how you speak, *señor!* This is my brand, and I—Don Tomás Topete—know how to make my knife and my gun talk to those who insult me."

The man who had said that the brand had been changed was a lean, long-jawed person in a wide hat. He looked as much like a typical *ranchero* as Don Tomás himself. Señor Lerdo, still puffing his cigar, stood beside him. Lerdo said quickly, "Don Tomás, this is Don Pedro Palma, who has a famous ranch in the State of Aguascalientes. He lost some fine bulls a short time ago. He believes that they were stolen and he is hunting all over Mexico hoping to find them before they are killed in the ring. He did not mean to insult you. He spoke from an anxious heart."

"Let him learn to keep his thoughts to himself then!" Don Tomás boomed.

Pedro Palma was a hard man. He looked Don Tomás in the eye, studied the stamping bulls for a moment, and said coolly. "From this distance, the brand looks to be changed."

"*Señor!*" Don Tomás roared. "This is my own brand! I warn you——"

A man in a leather jacket, whom Luis knew to be in charge of the bulls, stepped between the two ranchers. With a sharp sort of politeness, he said, "Gentlemen, the bulls will not come out the

183

gate so long as you stand here yelling at each other. If you want to settle the matter of the brand, why don't you step down into the *corral* for a close-up look?"

Of course anyone who tried to go into the *corral* to look at the brands on those bulls would have been killed in two minutes. The idea made the quarreling men seem foolish. The others on the platform roared with laughter. While the moment of good humor lasted, Señor Lerdo tugged at Pedro Palma's arm and got him to go downstairs.

A gasoline can filled with rocks came bouncing into the *corral* with a loud, rattling noise.

184

The bulls moved a few feet closer to the gate. The man who had thrown the can pulled it back by a lasso tied to it and threw it again. Luis was so interested that he barely noticed when Señor Lerdo came back, spoke in a low voice to Don Tomás, and went down the stairs leading the rancher by the arm.

Before very long the first of the bulls went through the gate. The others would follow. The best of the show was over, and Luis himself went down the stairs to look for a *taco* stand.

He was making his way around the arena when he heard his name called. Don Tomás came hurrying up to him.

The big rancher's forehead was covered with drops of sweat. Fear and worry had twisted his face into a knot. He handed Luis an envelope, and said

in a low, hoarse voice: "You must take this to Pidal. There is no one else I can trust. I have arranged for you to go in the cargo plane that leaves in twenty minutes. You will be taken in my car to the airport."

Don Tomás's thoughts untied the knot of worry that had twisted his face. He looked down at Luis gently, sadly. "Go with God," he said, and turned away.

As Luis came to the gate, a *matador* in tight-fitting, spangled clothes passed by. He was going to pray in the little chapel at one side of the bull ring.

The plane was just like the one that had brought Luis and the bulls. But it smelled of horses. One of the men who was fastening the cargo in place told Luis that the plane often carried fine horses down to the race track at Mexico City.

The workmen left, and the big plane thundered into the air. Luis was surprised to find that he was not afraid, this time. He caught sight of the sea, and the white houses of San Diego. Then there was nothing to see but clouds, and he took an interest in the cargo. Down both sides of the plane were stacked paper boxes holding women's clothes. But in the middle were two small, shiny racing cars—the most beautiful cars Luis had ever seen. He sat down in the red one and enjoyed himself until the plane began to jump and jerk in bumpy air.

Luis's stomach began to jump and jerk, also. He did not know until afterward that the pill the doctor had given him had kept him from being sick on the way up. Now he had no pill. He climbed out of the car, found a bucket that had been used to water horses, and was very sick.

Afterward, he lay on the floor, with his insides still jumping. The feeling that this trip was a bad dream came back and stayed with him all the way to Guadalajara. There were too many things he did not understand. Too many people were unhappy. And for once in his life, Luis had known too much excitement.

It was night when he finally climbed down, half-falling, onto the Guadalajara air field. Luis felt like kissing the ground. He felt as if he never wanted to leave again.

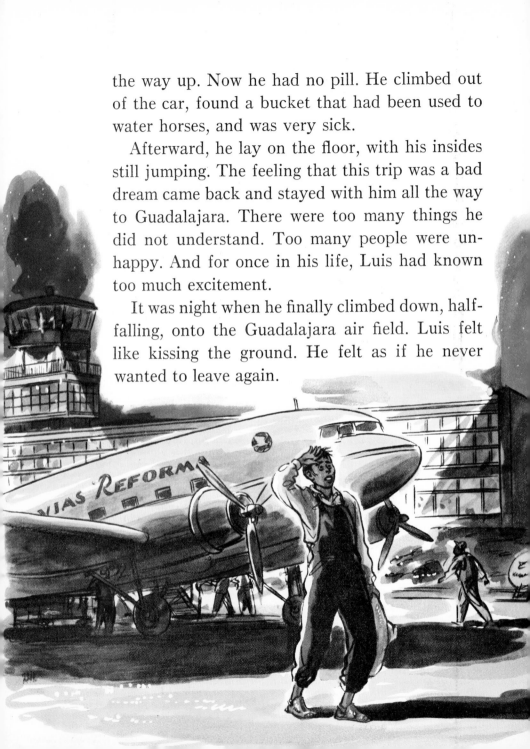

CHAPTER 15

The Hunt Through the Market

Luis was worried. The note from Don Tomás for Pidal was still in his pocket, and he did not know when he could see him. The night before, he had hitched a ride from the airport to Pidal's house. Pidal was not at home. The cook thought it best for him to stay there all night. But Pidal had not returned when Luis woke, late next morning. The cook fixed him an egg, and while he was eating it the telephone rang in another room.

When the cook came back from answering, she said, "Señor Pidal wants you to find the American businessman, Mr. Johnson. Ask him to come here about noon. Tell him it's important."

At Mr. Johnson's hotel they told Luis that Mr. Johnson had gone to the big market called *San Juan de Dios*. On his way there, Luis felt as if he had to hunt for a needle in a haystack. He was also worried for fear Mr. Johnson did not know Spanish. Luis was not sure that an American would understand the English he had learned in school.

As Luis drew near to the market building, the crowd grew thicker and thicker. It was more like a country crowd than a city crowd. Many of the men wore the old-style white pants, called *calzones,* which have no shape to speak of. The sound of feet on the pavement was the shuffle of sandals rather than the pounding of heels. Luis moved among the high, peaked hats of Jalisco, sometimes ducking under a wide brim perched on top of a short person. The faces of the women were almost hidden by the *rebozos* drawn close around them.

190

Here in the market of *San Juan de Dios,* the
country people flow into Guadalajara along with
the fruits and vegetables and flowers and hand-
made things that come from the villages. Some
of the people come only for the day. Luis could
recognize such folk by the way they stood in
front of the goods spread out beneath awnings.
They would stand a long time, uncurl their fists
to look at a few coins held in the palm, then
close their hands again and move on. They would

look and look, hunting the places where their money would go farthest. And after their money was spent they would go on drifting and looking for a long while.

There were men and women who looked just the same as the visitors, except that they were more busy and bustling. They seemed sure of themselves and knew where everything was. These were people who had come to live in the city but still wore country-style clothes.

There were many men, also, in work pants and T shirts and jackets of United States style, also women in cotton dresses of the kind housewives wear; also a few women dressed expensively in the latest styles, and men in business suits. Almost everyone in Guadalajara goes at one time or another to *San Juan de Dios.*

All these folk moved in and out of the background. But the tall figure topped by yellow hair which Luis was most anxious to get into the picture did not come in sight. Luis went inside the market and walked down a long aisle where roll after roll of bright cloth made a cheerfulness. There were all kinds of cloth—wool, cotton, linen, silk; some coarse, some fine; some made in factories by machines, and some made on hand looms. Much of this cloth had traveled only a few blocks to get to the market. Though most of the mills in Guadalajara are small, there are many of them. Together they spin and weave a good part of the cloth our people wear and some to sell in other places.

Even some Mexicans make the mistake of thinking that our markets are places where all the businesses are small, places where the people who sell goods earn barely enough to live on. In a big market like *San Juan de Dios*, there are businesses of all sizes. Some of the stalls Luis passed were very large. The cloth for sale in these had cost the owners thousands of *pesos*.* Some of the owners had more goods stored on the balcony which runs all the way around the huge room through which Luis was wandering. Looking up, he could see not only rolls of cloth but baskets of all sizes, shapes, and colors, mats of woven reeds, leather furniture, and in one corner a flock of bright *piñatas* hanging from the rafters.

---

* A *peso* is to us what a dollar is to you in the United States. One hundred *centavos* make one *peso;* a workman is paid about eight *pesos* a day.

Turning into another aisle, Luis passed through a strong-smelling section where soap and candles are sold. He passed neat piles of soap cakes just the right size for using and already wrapped in bright paper. But a lot of the soap was in bright-colored bars the size of stove wood. The people who sold it cut these bars into cakes for each customer.

Some of the candles were ordinary ones for lighting homes. These were mostly for country people, for Guadalajara itself has plenty of electricity. The thick candles which burn slowly were for anybody. Thousands of homes in our city have altars where people keep candles burning before a holy image or picture.

Beyond the candles, Luis came to stalls selling rope in coils and rope made into halters and bridles. Beyond were *ixtle* fibers. In many homes these coarse, whitish fibers are used for bathing. They are scratchy, and it feels good to wash with them. Some people use wads of *ixtle* for washing dishes. The fibers come from the tall, pointed leaves of maguey. The rope sold in our markets is made of maguey fibers, too.

Of course Luis looked at all these things as he passed by them. It would be a very dull person who could go through a market without being interested in what he saw—and in what he smelled; the market odors are mingled like the sounds from a hundred strange instruments. But all the while Luis was searching for the tall, yellow-topped figure of Mr. Johnson. Not finding him, he went out into a narrow street behind the market building.

Under the awnings which stretched from the wall out into the muddy street were pots and dishes enough for a thousand kitchens. This whole street was lined with pottery. Some of it was nested on the ground, and some stood on sloping racks against the building wall. Though most of it was the soft-looking pottery from the nearby towns, some stalls had the wares of states that border on Jalisco. Luis had been to many of the pottery towns with his father, and as he passed he said in his mind such names as Dolores Hidalgo (a famous place in the State of Guanajuato) and Tzintzuntzan, which is beside a lake in Michoacán. There was pottery from both these places and many others besides.

The day was very bright. The glazed dishes and bowls glistened like bubbles floating in the sunny air. But Luis liked best the kitchen pots. Their soft red-brown was so kind to the eyes, and their shapes were so comfortable to look at.

When he told my mother how he liked these pots, she laughed and nodded her head. "The kitchen pots have the beauty of a good, sweet wife," my mother said. "The glazed ones are like women with painted mouths and dresses that catch the eye. In a home, they do not look so pleasing as they do in the street."

Luis stopped long enough in the street of pottery to buy a boy with a watermelon and a woman with a market basket. These were for our model of the city. He stuffed the little figures into his pockets and hurried on.

Mr. Johnson was not in the street where wooden tubs and tin tubs and copper kettles are sold. He was not among the bird cages of tin that throw bright sparkles of sun into one's eyes. Luis turned into a street of shoes, which would lead him back into the big square in front of the market.

The smell of leather was all around him, though the shoe places were only on his right, across from the market building. These places are about the size of your garages, and have no fronts. They looked to Luis like a row of boxes standing side by side. "They would be easy to put into

our model," he thought. "We could simply cover small paper boxes with clay and get tiny toy shoes and *guaraches* to hang in the doorways.

It would be fun to do this," Luis thought—and the shoe places would look exactly as they looked to him as he passed by.

He saw hundreds of sandals, and also regular shoes of the kind you have, and also shoes woven of strips of leather, like baskets. Inside the box-like stalls men and boys were making these kinds of coverings for the feet. It was the fresh leather they used that gave the street its strong and curious smell. It is a smell one can find almost anywhere in the parts of Guadalajara where working people live. In hundreds of rooms and apartments families make shoes and sandals. They make many more than Guadalajara can wear. Each year we send thousands of pairs of shoes to the United States.

Luis was getting worried because he could not find Mr. Johnson. He turned away from the shoe places and hurried through the part of the market where food is sold. Another day he would have stopped to watch men cleaning the bright-colored fish that come from the Pacific Coast in cold railroad cars. He might have looked into the big cages of live chickens and ducks and other fowl, and stopped to chat with a butcher while he killed and cleaned a fowl for a waiting customer. But today he had no time for anyone by Mr. Johnson. Not finding him, he went quickly out. He was standing in the square, wondering where to look next, when a man came up to him and said, "What are you doing down this way, Luis?"

This man was dressed in a business suit, though not a very new or fine one. He had in his hand the kind of punch that bus drivers use to punch transfers. He used this to punch holes in the tickets our market merchants keep to show that they have paid their fees. His job was to collect the money which each person who has a stall in a market, and each person who sells in the street, must pay to the government of the city. The city owns the markets and rents space to the merchants.

Luis knew this collector of money well, for he had worked in the market in our own *barrio* up until a short time before. It did not seem wise to tell him anything of the business for Pidal. But meeting a man who worked for the city government reminded Luis that my father had asked him to find out whether people thought well enough of him to make him mayor. To Luis, this was much more important, even, than the message to Mr. Johnson. So he said, "I have been looking for little clay figures of people one sees in the streets. Martín, the son of Don Agustín Mendosa, is building a model of Guadalajara, and I am helping him."

"Don Agustín Mendosa!" said the collector. "There is a man Guadalajara should be proud of! Whenever there is work to be done for the good of the people, Don Agustín is one of the first to give his help. Without pay, too! And he does not forget his friends. Years ago, a friend of mine did Don Agustín a favor. Last Christmas time my friend was struck by an automobile. Don Agustín paid his bills at the hospital and saw to it that his family did not lack for anything. What do you think of that, now?"

Luis answered that my father was truly a fine man. While Luis was talking, the collector stopped a man who was going by with a big pack of folded *sarapes* strapped to his back. The collector took the man's money and punched a hole in a

small, white card which showed that the man had permission to sell *sarapes* on a certain street corner. When the collector turned back to Luis he had something else on his mind. He said, "If we could keep the peddlers off the streets and the cattle off the roads, one would have room to move in Guadalajara!"

It is true that the streets of our city are very crowded. Thousands of people come to the city each day to buy things they need, for Guadalajara is the center to which everything under the sun comes by railroad and highway and airplane. There are not stores and markets enough to sell to all the people from other towns and to those of us who live in the city as well. For this reason, the peddlers wander all over our downtown streets and storekeepers without stores set up little tables on the sidewalks.

Though most of the cattle we eat come by railroad, the small ranchers nearby still drive their animals to town along the roads, as they

have been doing for hundreds of years. Often they are a great danger to automobiles. Thinking of all this, Luis grinned and said, "If you took the cattle off the roads and the peddlers off the streets our city would be neat but it would not be Guadalajara!"

The collector laughed and started off to get the city's money from a man with a pushcart full of squashes.

"By the way," Luis called after him, "have you seen a tall American with yellow hair wandering around the market?"

"I have," the collector said. "He passed me not more than ten minutes ago and went across the square."

Having thanked him, Luis set out in the direction the collector's finger pointed. He crossed the square from corner to corner and found himself among open-air booths which sell hot meals. These booths are like small *corrales* with roofs over them. The cooking is done in the middle. The people who eat sit on benches around the sides. These booths are famous for their barbecues. When he smelled a whiff from roasting meat, Luis's stomach gave a gasp and a wriggle. It was not very long since breakfast, but any time is a good time to eat, when you are a boy. His feet took him toward the booth.

When he had ordered spareribs, Luis looked at the other people on the benches. A couple of men in T shirts were digging into their meat with a pleasure that made Luis grin. Next to them was a man who made him stare. He was big, he had blue eyes, his hair was yellow. He was Mr. Johnson.

He was looking at Luis. When he saw the small beginnings of a grin on Luis's face—a grin that was waiting to grow until he was sure that Mr. Johnson knew him—the American smiled. Luis leaned forward.

"Mr. Johnson," he said, speaking the English words very slowly and carefully, "Mr. Pidal would like to talk with you at noon, please."

Mr. Johnson spoke a lot of English words very fast. It seemed to Luis that he was saying that he would go to Señor Pidal's house. But Luis was not sure. He shook his head and said, in Spanish, "I do not understand."

The cook set a plate of spareribs down in front of Mr. Johnson. But he did not begin to eat right away. He said, "Let's see if my poor Spanish will do. It's lonesome to eat without anyone to talk to."

Luis found that by trying hard he could understand most of what Mr. Johnson said. Mr. Johnson, by trying even harder, could understand Luis, who talked slowly and used his hands to describe things. In this way he made Mr. Johnson understand that he had been to the bull ring. Mr. Johnson said that this was the third time he had been to *San Juan de Dios* market. He loved to wander around Guadalajara. He liked the food. He liked the people. He hoped that he could start a business in our city so that he could come to Guadalajara often.

The cooks listened and watched with smiling faces. The two young men in T shirts stopped eating to listen, and one of them joined in the talk between Luis and Mr. Johnson. Everyone had a good time, and Luis was rather sorry when he had finished his spareribs and it was time to go.

"Tell Señor Pidal," Mr. Johnson said, as he started away, "that I will be at his house in less than an hour."

It did not seem to Luis that Mr. Johnson was very pleased to be going to Pidal's. He wondered why.

The Big Lie

The house where Señor Pidal lived stood on a corner. As Luis hurried toward it, he saw a car dash up the cross street and come to a quick stop. The large figure of Don Tomás Topete got out of the car and walked with big steps to the front door. Luis broke into a run. They would be angry with him for being so late. If Señor Pidal had already gone, it would be very bad indeed.

The cook had a green silk handkerchief wrapped around her head and wore round, gold rings in her ears. She looked like a pirate when she came to the screen door. She gave Luis a slow, hard look and motioned him to come in, saying nothing.

In the kitchen a man stood leaning against a table, cleaning his gun. It was the small, flat kind of pistol that fits into the palm of a man's hand. Luis thought nothing of this. Many Mexicans own pistols, and a kitchen is as good a place as any for cleaning a gun. But the man himself was Manuel, the one who had stood guard beside Doña Josefa's door that day when Luis first met Pidal.

"*Buenas tardes* (good afternoon)," said Luis.

Manuel hooked his thumbs into his belt, holding the pistol in the fingers of his right hand. He spoke no word, but followed Luis with his brass-colored eyes. Once more he reminded Luis of a wolf.

The cook spoke to Manuel, and he answered in his husky, whispering voice. He had a very strong Spanish accent, lisping his words so much that Luis could hardly understand. This sounded silly to Luis, for we Mexicans do not lisp as most Spaniards do. Manuel was wearing a dark, tight-fitting shirt that came up all around his neck. It made him look foreign and funny. Even his fierce expression made Luis want to grin. They were both working for Pidal. Why should the man try to scare him?

From the way they spoke to one another, it seemed that Manuel and the woman were husband and wife. The sound of voices came from the next room. The cook said that Manuel should take Luis in, even though the boss had a visitor.

Manuel called her a bad name, but he opened the swinging door and Luis passed through, feeling uneasy because he was so late.

Don Tomás Topete was sitting at the table with Pidal, and he scowled at Luis like a thundercloud. Señor Pidal's eyes made him feel as if two cold stones were touching his face. Worse, he did not speak to Luis but simply left him standing there while he went on talking to the big *ranchero*.

"You are so excited I cannot understand you," Pidal said. "Speak slowly and calmly and tell me again. Why has Señor Lerdo come to Guadalajara?"

Don Tomás wiped his forehead with a red handkerchief. His big, strong hands were shaking. "The matter comes down to this: Señor Lerdo wants to be sure that the bulls he saw in Tijuana are not the bulls Pedro Palma is looking for. He will not pay the money until he has proof that the bulls were not stolen."

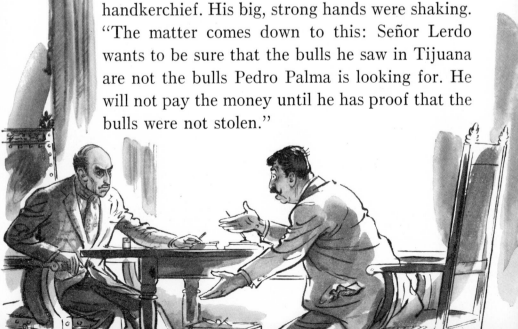

"What kind of proof does he want?" asked Pidal, making flame with a silver lighter and touching it to his cigarette.

"He will take Arturo Amador's word. When I told him that Don Arturo is my partner, he was almost ready to trust me right then. But Lerdo is a careful man. He will not have the bank pay over the money to us until he hears from Don Arturo himself."

"But this is very simple to manage!" Señor Pidal said. "Lerdo cannot talk with Don Arturo, because Don Arturo is out of the city. All that is needed is a letter to Lerdo with Don Arturo's name signed to it."

Don Tomás stared at Pidal. "You could manage to get Don Arturo's name on a letter?"

"Surely!" said Pidal. "I have a man who is very good at signing names."

Afterward, Luis felt very foolish that he had not then and there understood what these two were planning. But he was worried because Pidal paid him no attention. It seemed as if, somehow, he had lost out with this great gentleman. Luis still thought of him as that. He wanted Pidal to think well of him, even more than he wanted to work for him. It takes a great deal to change a boy's trust and liking once he has given them to a man.

"Such a letter would do the trick," Don Tomás said, shaking his head. "But it is not enough. This afternoon Señor Lerdo will look for Don Arturo at the bullfights but will not find him. It is not likely that Don Arturo will be back from his ranch for a day or two. And Señor Lerdo has to leave tonight for Mexico City. This would all be good, except for one thing—Señor Lerdo is going to send a telegram to Don Arturo if he does not find him before he leaves."

Señor Pidal looked down for a moment at the cigarette between his slim fingers. He had on a ring with a large, green stone. His sport coat was dark green, and he wore a brown silk scarf around his neck instead of a tie.

"It would be much better if I myself got this telegram instead of Don Arturo," said Pidal, and turned suddenly to run his eyes over Luis. "I might send the boy, here. He got into Doña Josefa's house most easily, even though Manuel was standing guard." He stopped speaking once more to study Luis. "Why were you so long in

210

coming back. What kept you. I am not paying you to play with the boys in the street."

Luis tried to smile but found the looks of the men too chilly for pleasant feelings.

"Mr. Johnson was not at his hotel," he said, hurrying the words. "I had to look all over the market for him. But I gave him your message, Señor Pidal! He will be here very soon."

Pidal made a motion with his head toward the kitchen. "Go in there and wait," he said.

As Luis passed through the swinging door, he heard Pidal say, "The boy is too new to be given such work. I am not quite sure of him yet."

Manuel had put away his gun but stood exactly where he had been before, with his thumbs hooked into his belt. He stared at Luis just as he had stared before, following him with his eyes. The cook was shelling peas at the kitchen table. She reached out one of her feet—on which she had pink bedroom slippers—and touched a stool in a corner. She was inviting Luis to sit down. As he pulled out the stool, the doorbell rang. Manuel went to answer it.

Before the door into the dining room had stopped swinging behind Manuel, Don Tomás

Topete came hurrying through. He looked neither right nor left but plunged out the back door, putting on his big hat as he went.

Manuel was back in a short time, but he did not come clear into the kitchen.

"Now we are going to have a good show," he said, standing in the doorway and holding the door open. "The American has come. Just watch the boss play with him the way a fisherman takes in a fish he has hooked."

The cook said in her grumbling voice, "How are we going to see anything? They're in the *sala*, aren't they? And we could not understand anything, even if we could hear. They'll be talking English."

"I can see through into the *sala*," Manuel said with an ugly grin. "And I learned English when I was smuggling whiskey into the United States."

Through the open door Luis could hear Mr. Johnson's strong voice and Pidal's smooth voice answering him. In a moment Manuel turned and said, "The American is telling how you found him in the market. Says he liked the food in that flytrap where he ate with you. No American knows anything about good cooking. The food in their cafes isn't fit for pigs!"

Manuel turned back to the open door. This time he listened longer.

"I didn't know the boss was so hard up," Manuel said. "He wants the American to give him ten thousand *pesos* right now. The American wants to know what he needs the money for. I'll give you ten to one the boss gets it."

To Luis it was like listening to a baseball game over the radio, with Manuel as the announcer.

"The boss is smart, smart! He doesn't tell him what the money is for. He goes round and comes up on the American's blind side. 'No American can understand Mexico,' the boss says. 'In the United States,' he says, 'you have mostly people of good European blood—Englishmen and Frenchmen, Germans and Italians. You killed off all the Indians long ago. But here in Mexico,

what have you got? Indians and half-breeds!' The boss says this like he was spitting. 'Mr. Johnson,' he says, 'these people here have the idea that they can run their own country. But they can't, of course. What does a simple savage or a half-breed know about modern law or business?' "

Manuel stopped again to listen. Luis was beginning to get over the first shock of surprise and his neck prickled with anger. Manuel spoke again. It was almost as if he smacked his lips with pleasure. "Mr. Johnson says that he has met some Mexicans, like Arturo Amador, who seemed very intelligent. He says he likes Mexicans. Imagine!" Here Manuel looked slyly at Luis. "The boss is explaining how things really are. He says the Mexicans are like children. Even those who seem bright are not up to making laws or running a business or doing anything that takes education. How truly he speaks! He says that the Mexicans must have their lives managed for them, whether they like it or not. It is the duty of the smart, civilized people of the world to manage them. They were much better off when Spain owned Mexico.

"How beautifully Señor Pidal speaks! 'Spare the rod and spoil the child,' he tells Mr. Johnson. He goes on to say that the Mexicans have become spoiled children since they won their freedom from Spain. They ought to be forced to let smarter people manage them. But the United States is the only country near enough and strong enough to force the Mexicans. And the United States will not send soldiers to make the Mexicans behave."

This was the first time Luis had come up against the way some foreigners feel about Mexico. For hundreds of years the Spaniards told the world that we Mexicans were children and fools. Some people still believe it, or pretend to believe it so that they will have an excuse for breaking our laws and taking all they can get from our country. But Luis had never before met this way of thinking face to face. Pidal had him gasping. Luis's neck burned with anger and his nails dug into his palms.

Manuel turned from his listening, with a smirk for Luis and a wink for the cook. "Now comes the good part!" he said. "Señor Pidal explains to the American that the Mexicans make laws as if they were children playing a game. They do business the same way. It would be hopeless to try to get anywhere with such a plan as Mr. Johnson has if one took the Mexicans seriously. The hope for Mr. Johnson's glass factory is that the Mexicans know in their hearts that their laws are not meant to be obeyed. They know that they can only pretend to be business-men but cannot really do business. The wise ones among the Mexicans are willing to work with a smart foreigner who gets things done but lets them go on pretending to be great makers of laws and captains of business. To put on this show costs money. But it is worth it.

" 'This is where people like me come in,' the boss explains. 'You Americans do not have the experience. You do not understand how to manage peasants and savages. It takes someone from an old, civilized country to do that.' He goes on to explain how he grew up in an old, old castle. For miles around, the peasants looked up to the Pidals and obeyed them and depended on them. Besides, Señor Pidal explains, he is part Spanish and part Italian. Spain and Italy have ruled over savages for a long time in Africa. It is in the

Pidal blood to manage low-class people. To get the glass factory started, Mr. Johnson must get someone to manage the Mexicans for him. Our boss is ready to start doing this the minute Mr. Johnson gives him the ten thousand *pesos,* and he knows how to spend them where they will do the most good."

The sound of voices from the other room grew lower. Manuel pushed a little farther through the door. When he turned to the kitchen again, he was laughing.

"Mr. Johnson wanted to know if the boss planned to do anything that is against the law. The boss said, 'No, not exactly. But we may have to get around some laws, Mr. Johnson.' "

Luis could stand no more. Before the two in the kitchen knew what he was about, he had wriggled past Manuel and was running across the dining room toward the *sala.* Mr. Johnson sat in a big armchair covered with green leather. Luis brought up before the American's surprised face and took a deep breath to steady himself.

"He lies!" Luis said, pointing toward Pidal. "Every word he has said is a big lie! We have good laws! We are not stupid. Right here in Guadalajara are many Mexicans so much better than Señor Pidal that he is not fit to shine their shoes. I will take you to one of them this very afternoon!"

The surprised look had gone from Mr. Johnson's face. He was frowning with his forehead, but he began to smile with his mouth. The frown was because he did not understand all Luis said. The smile was because he understood enough to feel sympathy with Luis.

218

Señor Pidal had gotten to his feet. He said, "Mr. Johnson, I apologize. This nasty boy has been listening to our talk like a little sneak! But what can you expect of a Mexican? Take him away, Manuel."

Strong hands took Luis's arms from behind and twisted them so that it was all he could do to keep from crying out. Manuel turned him around, marched him back to the kitchen, and set him on the stool. The grip the man kept on Luis's arm hurt. But the tears that stood in Luis's eyes were tears of anger.

CHAPTER 17

"Go, Little Fly!"

Luis was not kept on the stool for very long. He heard the front door close. Manuel ordered the cook to go to Pidal, and she came back saying that the *señor* wanted the boy.

It surprised Luis very much to find Pidal sitting at the dining-room table and looking just as he had before. From his face and the tone of his voice, one would have thought nothing had happened. He ran his shiny brown eyes over Luis, as if Luis were a toad. It would have been less frightening if he had roared with anger.

Luis stood straight and gave Pidal look for look.

"There are a number of things I might do with you—if it were worth my trouble to give you what you deserve," Pidal said. "But I'm busy. If I should let you go, what would you do?"

"I would go to Arturo Amador!" said Luis, breathing hard. "I'd get him to find Mr. Johnson and tell him——"

220

"Shut him up, Manuel," Pidal said, and the man clamped his hand over Luis's mouth. "That shows you are—a Mexican." Pidal said this as if "Mexican" were the worst thing he could think of to call a person. "We will have to put you where you can't talk. The police will be glad to lock up a little sneak whom we have caught stealing a billfold from my bedroom, eh, Manuel?"

What Manuel was about to say became lost in his yell. The yell was caused by Luis's teeth sinking into his finger to the bone. Luis started to run. But Manuel was quick. His swinging fist caught Luis on the side of the head and knocked him spinning into a corner.

The thing Manuel and Pidal did not know was that Luis had been kicked by many a burro and had learned a trick or two. He was moving away from the fist when it struck, and he managed to cover his head with his arms before he banged up against the wall. He was shaken and hurt. But he could still see and hear clearly.

Manuel took the telephone from a small table and set it on the big table. Señor Pidal asked the operator for the police station, not bothering to give the number. Manuel glanced down at Luis, who lay in a still, crumpled heap just as he had fallen. The way he looked seemed to satisfy Manuel, for he turned to Pidal, who now explained politely and pleasantly to the police that he had a little thief in his house.

"You will send a car right away?" he asked. "Good! Thank you very——"

Whether he finished the sentence or not, Luis never knew. For Luis had sprung to his feet. He darted through the swinging door and flung it back. There came a dull sound, as if it had hit Manuel in the face.

On the porch he saw the cook coming toward him with her arms full of dry dish towels ready for ironing. Luis thought he could dodge around her.

As he ran closer, he saw to his great surprise that she was smiling. Her strange eyes looked almost loving as she put her free hand behind her and opened the screen door.

"Go, little fly!" she said softly as he passed, "Yes indeed, fly away!"

Across the garden was a high, thick hedge. Luis dove into it like a scared rabbit and began to work his way through. He came out into the side street with his face scratched and his shirt torn. He now had to do something much harder than standing up to Pidal or making his escape from the house. These things he had done in anger, without thinking. Now he had to make himself walk calmly along the street. If he ran, people would notice him; when the police came asking who had seen a strange boy, they would tell where he had gone. But his pounding heart was saying, "Run, run, run!" and to keep control of his legs was one of the hardest things Luis could remember doing.

Finally he came to the corner and turned it. A high garden wall hid him from view, and he felt much safer. He walked boldly to the street where the busses ran. In the little knot of people waiting to get on the bus was a fat woman carrying two huge bunches of flowers. Luis took a place at her side. Far up the street a bus was coming.

"*Señora,*" Luis said to the woman, "it is going to be hard for you to get on the bus with those flowers. Please let me help you with them."

The woman clutched the flowers to her as if she were afraid he would steal them. But when she looked down into Luis's face she held one of the bunches out to him. Only a person very hard of heart could look at Luis's grin and doubt that he is truly friendly.

When a police car came cruising down the street, the policeman looking left and right, Luis had his face buried among bright pink gladioli.

"You monkey!" the flower woman scolded. "Gladioli don't smell."

"I just wanted to make sure, *señora,*" Luis said humbly.

He held the flowers in front of his face all the way to the great square beside the cathedral, where the busses stopped. The woman was going to the flower market behind the cathedral. Luis walked with her until they were beyond the two policemen who stood watching the people get off the busses. Then he gave back the gladioli and went around to the side of the great church, where one would scarcely know it is a church at all. On that side are long stretches of blank wall and a few shops.

He did not think that it was safe to go home yet. Pidal knew his name and the neighborhood where he lived. He would have told the police just what Luis looked like.

Luis should have come straight to our house and told my father everything, but the thought of having the police come looking for him at our house was more than Luis could bear.

The safest place he could think of was the cathedral tower. Luis ducked through a narrow door and made his way along a dark, stone-paved hall. He had the luck to find the door to the narrow, steep stairway open.

CHAPTER 18

High Above the City

There goes Luis, climbing first in light and then in darkness. Above the first, broad landing the stairway grows narrower and more steep. No wires carry electricity up there. The stairway is dark as a night without stars, except on the little landings where windows like slits let in stripes of light.

To come out onto the open balcony where the great bells hang is like climbing out of a tunnel stood on end. Luis slips between the bells and stands near the edge. He looks toward Zapopan,

226

the village where our famous Madonna stays when she is not making the rounds of the city churches.

There is nothing but empty air between the city and himself, and it seems to Luis that he can see it truly for the first time in his life.

Guadalajara is too big and beautiful and strong for any person to spoil its life, no matter how bad he may be. Even to be poor—to live in a crowded room and sometimes go hungry—does not make life bitter in our city. For to live in Guadalajara is to belong to it as a child belongs to its family. Each person shares our city's feelings and its doings. And because the city is good, life is good, unless one turns against the city as a bad son turns against his family.

This feeling comes to Luis as he looks out across the carpet of pale yellow-brown houses with their red roofs. He sees that Guadalajara is like the jewel in the center of a great brooch. Around it is a wide circle of green stretching away to the deep-blue sky. Luis has crossed this circle many times; he knows that one can walk steadily behind the burros for hours and hours and all the while the meeting place of sky and earth

moves ahead, keeping its distance. He knows that the sharp-edged hills to the south are higher and farther away than they look. Beyond them lies Lake Chapala, blue-gray like smoke, speckled here and there with the sails of fishermen's canoes.

The living green of the circle is grass, the summer clothing of the Guadalajara plain. Between the city and the nearest hills are clumps of darker green trees, with the red and brown of houses below them. These are the pottery-

making towns, with queer names which are part
Indian and part Spanish — San Pedro Tlaquepaque, the most famous of them all, and Tonalá
and Santa Cruz de las Vueltas.

To the east the lion-colored houses fade into
the rich green of cornfields. Beyond the fields the
green grows pale, mounting toward steep slopes.
Between the green of fields and the green of the
open plain is a slit in the earth, a canyon so deep
that the bottom has different weather from the

229

top. Luis cannot make out this canyon from the tower, but he knows where it is very well, having crossed it many times. We call this deep canyon *La Barranca de Oblatos*. This name is long and so I will shorten it to *Barranca*. This word has about the same meaning you have given to "canyon," which is a Spanish word, by the way.

When Luis thinks of the *Barranca* his thoughts seem to tumble over the steep side and roll to the bottom. Arturo Amador will be crossing the *Barranca* sometime within the next day or two. The ranch to which he has gone lies in that direction, at the foot of the mountains. He will be coming on horseback; the road cannot be traveled by any wheels.

As he thinks of Don Arturo, Luis begins to see the talk he heard at Pidal's and at the bull ring in a new way. When he thought that Pidal was a great gentleman and Don Tomás an honest rancher, he had given everything he heard a good meaning. Now Pidal has shown his true self, and Luis sees that bad meanings are probably the right ones.

"Suppose the bulls Don Tomás was trying to get Señor Lerdo to pay for have really been stolen?"

230

Luis asks himself. Luis answers himself, "Yes." Pidal's plan begins to unfold in Luis's mind. The bullfighters had surely killed the bulls soon after he had left Tijuana. So no one can tell whom they truly belonged to. But Señor Lerdo will not pay, unless he has proof that Don Tomás was their real owner. So—here Luis gives himself a slap for being stupid—so Pidal will write a letter to Lerdo and get a man who is clever with a pen to sign Don Arturo's name. But they must keep Don Arturo from getting Lerdo's telegram, so Pidal will have someone steal it from Don Arturo's house. This stealing must be the work for which Pidal said Luis was not yet ready.

Luis beats his fist into his hand so hard that the pigeons fly up from the great bells and sail away. He is so angry he talks out loud, calling Pidal names, but not forgetting to blame himself. "Very, very right was my father! I am a burro, with a thick hide and thick head. The only way I ever get any sense into my head is when somebody knocks it in."

As he speaks to himself, Luis puts his hand up to his cheek; the place where Manuel hit him is swollen and very, very tender. This, he thinks, is not the worst Manuel can do. The little flat gun he was cleaning in the kitchen is not a toy.

Luis could, of course, have gotten help from my father that very night. But he thinks of my family as being above the world's evil. We do not come into his mind at this time. Luis begins to think of something he can do himself. And as he thinks he smiles.

Soon he glances at the sun. It will not grow dark for another hour—a long wait. But he feels sure that Pidal has set the police to looking for him. Better to come down from the tower after dark. Luis sits down to wait with his back against the warm stones of an arch at the edge of the balcony. But sitting still is something Luis can never do for long. He wanders across to the other side of the balcony and stands looking down on the beating heart of Guadalajara. At the foot of the cathedral is a small, green park. In the street beyond stands a long row of carriages, the horses hanging their sleepy heads over the sidewalk. Behind the horses, automobiles flow in a

steady stream. And beyond the cars, people are flowing through the *portales*—the ever-moving, never-hurrying crowds of Guadalajara.

In this part, close around the cathedral, all the life of the city seems to start and make its way outward. Here men come to find out what they should buy or sell. Here it is decided what teachers shall teach, and what preachers shall preach. Here the policemen come to find out what they must do to keep the city safe each day. The gardeners and water-supply men and others who keep the city beautiful and healthful come here for their orders. From here the telephone calls go out to thousands of people who need to know what is going on and what they had best do.

To this part of the city comes the news, and it goes out again in stacks of newspapers and over the air on radio waves. The moving pictures come in their flat cans, and the people pour into the large theaters to watch them. Here men make business plans that give work to thousands in Guadalajara's factories.

As Luis looks down, he notices something that excites him because it will help with our model. The center of Guadalajara is like a puzzle made of odd-shaped pieces. Each piece has in it an old church, which is the thing people remember when they think of that particular part of town. "All we have to do," thinks Luis, "is build these churches into our model and people will be able to imagine the rest."

A few blocks south of the cathedral is a very old church called San Francisco. In the early times missionaries from all over the north of Mexico came there to rest and study and talk together.

Near the church of San Francisco are banks and the offices of many companies and Guadalajara's larger hotels. There are stores, too—but this is mainly a part of town for doing business rather than for shopping.

It is a part of town for walking and looking in the sunshine, also. Just in front of the church of San Francisco is the loveliest garden in Guadalajara. It is a double garden. I mean it is two whole city squares with streets all around and a street dividing them down the middle. The church itself is the color of wheat grains. It is very simple, as the churches of good St. Francis are meant to be. But its tower and walls and windows go so beautifully together that it is one of the most perfect buildings in North America.

Going around to the west, Luis's eyes pick out the church of Santa Mónica. This is a famous church, because of the carved stone. Even the stone grapes seem to have life in them. The large saint standing at the corner seems to bless you with a tender look each time you pass by. And in a courtyard next door are stone carvings so perfect that it is called the court of angels. The workmen who built this court (it was very long ago) disappeared every day just at the time they were to be paid. This was a great mystery until someone discovered that the workmen were angels, who simply flew home to heaven each evening. This is the story they tell of the church of Santa Mónica; many people in Guadalajara believe it.

Near the church of Santa Mónica is a large and crowded market, like the others I've told you about. Here also are the fancy grocery stores and the drugstores and other places where the richer people can get what they want—things a little finer and a little fancier, and things that are new to Mexico, such as washing machines and pure medicines.

Going west beyond Santa Mónica, Luis's eyes rest for a moment on the green trees and shining houses of the new *colonia* where Señor Pidal's house stands. He does not look at it long, but swings his eyes round to San Francisco again. Luis can barely make out the railroad station just behind the old church. The station is crowded, small, and noisy, always full of people looking a little worried as they wait for trains. Perhaps we will have a new railroad station some day. But perhaps not. Now that we have planes and busses, we use trains mostly for carrying things, not people.

From where Luis stands, this part of the city seems a jumble of roofs and streets. But he knows that it is not. It is busy and bustling around there, not shining nor exactly pretty. This part of town is like a man working hard, wearing work pants and work shirt, a little dirty and a little sweaty. It is a part of town where hard work is done.

The railroad runs on down till it comes to Independence Avenue. This is a street that cuts slantwise across the city. It is the street where things needed for work, rather than for just living, are brought to be sold. This is the street to come to if you want to buy a tractor or a pump, or a mill for grinding corn, or office furniture, or machines that add and subtract and multiply. Here men come to get their machinery repaired, to buy iron or copper or seeds to plant.

We have three railroads. One goes to Mexico City, leaving Guadalajara on the east side. This road is joined by a line to Texas. The other two railroads leave the city on the west side. One goes straight to the coast, to the port of Manzanillo. The other line turns northward and goes angling up the west side of Mexico. The end of this line is really Los Angeles, in California.

All along the tracks of these railroads, in the city and on its edges, are factories. Many of them are new and have very up-to-date machinery. They make oil for cooking and for manufacturing; also soap; also such new things as wallboard pressed from cornstalks; also sugar products, such as the bottled colas and fruit-flavored drinks we Mexicans love even more than you Americans do.

Luis swings around till he is facing east. There rises the tower and roof of the church of San Juan de Dios, the church that gives the great market its name. Over beyond it, to the left, is the bull ring.

It would tire you if I told everything that Luis saw. It tired Luis to see it. He sat down and watched the colors in the sky as the sun sank. When it was quite dark, he felt his way down the stairs, slipped through the silent hall and out into the street. It was quite dim in the street, and there was no one near except one man who was walking briskly toward Luis.

As Luis stood wondering which way would be best to go, a car turned the corner and threw a flood of light on both Luis and the man. It made the silver badge on the man's coat shine brightly. Luis was face to face with a policeman.

CHAPTER 19

We Hunt for Luis

It was about the time Luis came down from the tower that we began to worry about him. I had been very busy on the model all day; I finally got the *barrio* church finished and did some work on Luis's *vecindad*. I missed him, and when he did not turn up for two whole days, I got mad because I thought he had gone off on some adventure of his own, forgetting both me and the model. But we did not begin to worry until Raquel came, after dark.

In the cool of the early evening, my mother and father were having an iced drink and talking about my sister, Lucía, who had left that day by air. My mother does not trust airplanes much, but my father does. I was throwing small green berries through the kitchen door at Isabela. I did this because I was bored and wished to stir up some excitement. Before I could get her angry by landing a berry in the meat-ball soup, the knocker boomed on the door.

I raced Anselmo across the patio and beat him. I could not see Raquel's face at the door, but her voice sounded most anxious.

"Oh, Martín!" she said. "Is Luis here?"

I said he had not come that day and I was angry with him.

"You must not talk that way! Is your mother at home?"

I took Raquel to my mother and father, wondering greatly what had upset her. It was hard to wait until the grownups had all said polite how-do-you-dos and Raquel sat down.

"I'm frightfully worried!" Raquel's warm voice was so low I could barely hear what she said. "Perhaps I'm just being a silly woman, but I can't help feeling that something dreadful has happened to Luis. Coming home from work, I met his old godmother. I asked her if it wasn't lonely having Luis and his father both away, and she said——"

My father stopped Raquel to say that we had not known that Luis and his father had planned to go away. Raquel explained how they had both come to her house two nights before and how Don Sebastián had planned to go off on an egg-buying trip that morning.

"Don Sebastián left, but Luis did not go with him!" Raquel said. "His godmother says that Luis left the house by himself early this morning and hasn't come back since."

My mother grew upset, too. She said she did not know what in the world she would do if I were missing for a whole day. I remembered what Luis had said about being one of the "burros of this world," meaning that he was not watched over so carefully as myself.

"I think Luis can take care of himself," I said.

"Martín is right," said my father. "It is a good guess that the boy went out to the bull ring and spent the day there."

In a little while Raquel went home feeling a good deal better. My father is very good at calming people down. But after I got into bed, I began to imagine all sorts of things that might have happened to Luis. While I was sick, I had been too much alone. It was easy for my mind to turn the world into a comic-book place and frighten myself half to death. Before I went to sleep, I had seen Luis being chased through the streets by a mad bull; I had watched him take off for the moon in a one-man rocket ship; I had

242

suffered while a man with corkscrew mustaches hypnotized him. My father heard me tossing in my bed and came in.

"Go to sleep!" he said, giving me a firm pat. "If Luis does not turn up in the morning, we will go and find him."

My father keeps his promises. When he came home at noontime and Luis still hadn't showed himself, we set off at once for the *vecindad*.

When we walked into the big courtyard, it was like entering a place where I had been before. Luis had told me so much about it that even the patches where plaster had chipped away from the building stone seemed familiar. The men were away, except for the young fellow who wanted to play with the *mariachis* (traveling street musicians). Down in the far corner, his guitar stopped with a twang as my father and I crossed the patio through the dazzling

light. Several women looked up from their cooking to watch us, and children began coming out
of doorways.

Luis's godmother came shuffling out of the
room where they lived and made an old-
fashioned curtsy to my father. She seemed to
think it would serve Don Sebastián right if
something had happened to Luis. She muttered
on and on about how, if Don Sebastián would
stop lending money to every Tom, Dick, and
Harry and give Luis a decent home such things
would not happen.

While the old woman talked on, children of
many different sizes gathered around. One or
two of them ran off to tell their mothers. From
all over the *vecindad,* women came to join us.

"Luis lost?" they asked. "Missing since last
night? May the good God let nothing bad
happen to him!" They were very much upset.

From what Luis had said of her, I recognized Magdalena, the young mother who was so cross when her husband went away. She was a tall woman with bold eyes and a good deal of lipstick. She did not look like one who has a tender heart. Yet she seemed to feel worse than any of the others. She kept telling the young guitar player that he must go at once to look for Luis and not come back until he had found him.

"I'll go as soon as I change my clothes," he said, and left us.

The last to arrive was the wife of Don Bartolo, the man who works on a garbage truck. She came down the patio with her children running ahead of her, like a mother quail with a brood of chicks. As Luis had said, they were a clean, nice-looking family. The baby grinned and jumped in his mother's arms. All the women talked at once, telling her about Luis.

"But I know where he went!" said Don Bartolo's wife. "He stopped to play with the baby on his way out, and he said he was going to see a rich *señor*. His name was——" She stopped and put her hand to her forehead, thinking. I nearly died of the strain while she tried to remember. "I think Luis was going to ask him for a job. His name began with *P*. Was it Pino? No! Pidal!" She turned to my father with a happy smile.

"I will go to see this gentleman," my father said. "Thank you, *señora*."

My father had a business meeting, so it was late afternoon when he finally got to Pidal's house. Señor Pidal seemed very friendly. He said he had heard that my father was going to run for mayor of Guadalajara. My father would make a fine mayor, Pidal said. He went on praising the Mexican laws and the Mexican businessmen, saying that everything was much better in our country than in the old countries of Europe.

It seemed to my father that Pidal was spreading the butter on too thick. He made no answer to the man's flattery but said he had come to ask about a boy named Luis.

Pidal did not remember the name. What did Luis look like? When my father described him, Pidal said that he remembered Luis perfectly. He had been amused at the way Luis got into Doña Josefa's. But he had not seen Luis since. Had something happened to him?

246

You can believe that I was a very sad boy when my father came home and told me what Pidal had said. I could not keep my mind on the model nor even eat more than three of the little cakes Isabela brought to cheer me up.

It began to grow dark. The noise of automobiles bringing people home from work faded from the street. The house was still and the *barrio* was still. Into the stillness came sounds of men talking outside our house and odd little twangs of strings and the running notes of a violin. This was followed by a knock on our door. I went with Anselmo.

Outside stood a band of *mariachis* in their tight pants and short jackets and big hats. They had their violins and guitars and horns in their

hands. The young guitar player who lived in Luis's *vecindad* was standing in front of our door. He had his hat off. His face was most serious as he looked at me and said, "Tell your father that Luis was seen early yesterday afternoon in *San Juan de Dios* market. He talked with an American named Señor Johnson. *Adiós.*"

When I told my father this, he took the telephone book from its place beside the desk in his study. He began calling hotels and asking if a Mr. Johnson was stopping there. The clerk in the third hotel said yes. As he talked to Mr. Johnson a look of surprise came to my father's face. When he finally said good-by, he laid the telephone down very gently, as he does when he is angry. "Mr. Johnson says that Luis was at Pidal's yesterday afternoon! He is coming here to talk to us about Luis and Pidal. He says there are things going on that he does not understand."

I was not used to the ways of Americans at that time. It surprised me that Mr. Johnson got to our house so quickly; it seemed as if my father had barely put the telephone down before he was knocking at our door. Anselmo brought him to the porch where I was sitting with my father and mother. I liked the way Mr. Johnson shook hands with me. My father, of course, speaks English very well. Though I did not understand so much of your language as I do now, I knew what my father was saying when he explained to Mr. Johnson that I was a special friend of Luis.

"I have a boy about his age," Mr. Johnson said. "I think Martín would like to hear what his friend did yesterday afternoon. It made me proud to know Luis—even though we have just met."

So we sat down in the comfortable chairs on the porch and Mr. Johnson told us how Luis had come in to tell him that Pidal lied. It took a while for him to get to that part because he had first to tell us a little about his plan for a glass factory, and how he came to know Pidal. Isabela and Anselmo came to stand in the shadows. As the story grew more exciting, they edged toward the table, until we made one listening group.

My father did not say anything, but my mother and Isabela exclaimed often. Once or twice I heard Anselmo say what he would like to do with Pidal.

"What I have been wondering ever since you telephoned," Mr. Johnson said, "is whether Pidal has Luis shut up somewhere in his house."

"I do not think so," my father said thoughtfully. "Pidal seems to be very smart. He would make sure that no one can prove that he had anything to do with the fate of Luis."

Mr. Johnson said that if Pidal had done something bad and they could find it out, Pidal could be made to tell the truth.

My father said, "I have been trying to think who told me about Pidal some time ago. It must have been Gonzalo de la Cruz. His family was great and rich and powerful in Spain for hundreds of years. Now they have nothing left but their honor. Don Gonzalo went to France just before the Second World War and stayed to fight with the French underground army against the Germans. Now he has come over here and makes his living taking photographs. A good man, if ever there was one."

250

My father got to his feet. "I think I will telephone to Don Gonzalo and ask about Pidal. With your permission?"

Mr. Johnson seemed so friendly and nice that I wanted to do something for him. The thing I thought of to do was to show him my model. Afterward, it surprised me that I trusted him so much. I was quite shy about showing the model to anyone, because it was important work to me. I could not bear to have anyone treat our model as little-boy business.

Mr. Johnson praised it very much. He said that when it was done I should take some pictures of it. He wanted to have the pictures to show his own son what Guadalajara really looks like.

My father came back saying that the operator in Mexico City would call him if she was able to locate Gonzalo de la Cruz. Isabela had brought a pitcher of *jamaica*—the sweet drink made of red flowers. Mr. Johnson was most pleased with the way it tasted.

"I like everything about Guadalajara," he said. "I can't say exactly why, any more than you can say just why you like some people on sight. But

251

the real reason I thought of starting a glass factory here is because I fell in love with your city.

"I tell you, I was about ready to give up and go home yesterday afternoon when Pidal was talking. The man is wonderful with words. He had me halfway believing that there was something about Mexico I couldn't understand. I thought to myself that if I had to do what he said—work with somebody like Pidal who knew his way around among you Mexicans—I didn't want to do business here. I like to trust the people I work with.

"I should have seen through him days ago. But it is easy to fool a stranger in a strange land. When Luis came in and called him a liar, it woke me up. It's as plain as the nose on your face that you people who have made Guadalajara what it is can't be children or fools. And that Luis! He's still a boy—but he talked and acted like a man yesterday."

My father's voice was so low and steady that only my mother and I knew how strong were the feelings coming out in his words.

"Mr. Johnson," he said, "I must admit to you that we Mexicans are not always easy to get along with. The reason is that we have suffered too much from men like Pidal. They have been coming over here ever since Cortez conquered our country—like wolves to a sheep pasture. At best, they have treated us like children, and at worst they have treated us like work animals. They have taken the gold and silver from our mines. They have made us labor for them in fields that were once our own. Worst of all, they have made the world believe the great lie that Mexicans are not fit for anything but guitar playing, flirting, horseback riding, and hard labor with the hands.

"The other day," my father said, turning toward me, "this boy of mine butted a guest in the stomach. It was a rude, bad thing to do. Yet in a way the boy was right. The guest was trying to take over the boy's model of Guadalajara and make it his own. The guest wished to say how the model should be built—leaving only the handwork to Martín. My son felt that he had no right to do this.

"We Mexicans feel the same way about our country. It is ours. No one has a right to take it away from us. We feel that we Mexicans can do any work that other people do—brainwork as well as handwork. We have not had our freedom long, and we lack what you call know-how. We often make mistakes, but we will fight for our right to make mistakes. Men as well as boys can learn only by trying."

There was a silence when my father's voice stopped. Then Mr. Johnson said, "Does what you say mean that you would not want me to start a glass factory here?"

"By yourself, no. With us Mexicans as partners, yes. A thousand times, yes! We need factories. We will do all we can to help along a project like yours. You have seen the big, new store near the cathedral?"

Mr. Johnson nodded.

"This store shows exactly what I mean, Mr. Johnson," my father went on. "This store—and its brother stores in other cities—are run by your people and mine, working together. And together they are making a great deal of money. Our people love those stores! They have helped thousands of Mexicans to live better."

I forgot that a child is not supposed to break into grown-up talk. A question had been in my mind for a long time, so I asked it. "What makes

254

the big, new store so different from our other stores?" I wanted to know. "Everybody talks about how you can be sure of getting the most for your money there. I want to know why."

I saw Mr. Johnson's smile gleam in the half-darkness of the porch. "Are you good in arithmetic, Martin?"

"He is very good!" said my mother.

"All right," said Mr. Johnson, "suppose you are an old-fashioned storekeeper. You can sell only 100 shirts a month. But you must make $400 on shirts each month in order to pay your rent and your clerks. Shirts cost you $1.00 each. How much must you sell them for?"

I worked the answer out in my head and told it to Mr. Johnson.

"Now," said Mr. Johnson, "suppose you are one of the owners of the new store. You also must make $400 each month on shirts. But you can sell 1,000 shirts a month. The factory lets you have them cheaper because you buy so many. You pay 75 cents each—$750 for a thousand. How much must you sell them for to make $400?"

To get the answer to this one I had to go to my room and figure with a pencil and paper.

255

When I came back, my father was at the door talking to some men. Mr. Johnson praised me for getting the answer to the problem of the shirts. He said, "This is what makes the new store different. The old stores must make a great deal on each thing they sell. The new store needs to make only a little on each thing it sells. This is one big reason why people in the United States are able to have plenty to eat and good clothes to wear and nice automobiles to ride in."

When my father came back to us, he brought five men with him. They stood with their big hats in their hands, very quiet and polite. But the feeling of anger had come in with them.

My father said in English, "These are Luis's neighbors, who have come to get the news. They are now going out to hunt for Luis. If he is not found by tomorrow night, half the people in this *barrio* will be looking for him. We all feel as if we had lost a well-loved member of the family."

He told the men Mr. Johnson's name. Don Bartolo stepped forward and in a very dignified way said the polite words that have been our custom for hundreds of years. "Don Bartolo Sereno, at your service!" He shook hands with Mr. Johnson. The others said the same words. They were the plumber, the seller of herbs, and the baker, who live in Luis's *vecindad*—also Magdalena's husband, who now had a job putting gasoline in the tanks of planes when they light at our airports. My father told them about Luis and Pidal.

"I'm glad to have met them," Mr. Johnson said when they had gone.

"I thought you would be," said my father. "These are humble men who have little education. But they work hard and honestly for their living, and they can be good friends—as you see!"

"I would not like to be Pidal and meet any of these men tonight!" Mr. Johnson said. "You know, this is kind of strange—the way Luis is bringing us all together. I feel as if I'd become part of Guadalajara for a little while. It's a good feeling!"

"I hope you are going to be still more one of us," my father said. "It has been in my mind for a long time that we ought to build an up-to-date glass factory here. Would you care to tell me just what you had in mind?"

My mother said that business talks were no place for women and children. She hurried me off to bed.

CHAPTER 20

We Learn More About Pidal, and I Visit the Toymakers

I was putting on my clothes next morning when I heard the knocker booming on our door. I looked out my bedroom door and saw Anselmo bring in a square, strongly-made man wearing blue overalls and a jacket of the same cloth. It seemed certain that he had come about Luis, so I hurried.

"This is Don Sebastián, Luis's father," my father said when I came up to them where they stood in the patio.

We Mexicans do not often shake hands hard; it is the custom to touch the hands firmly but very lightly—as Don Sebastián now touched mine. Yet I could feel the strength and hardness of his hand. He gave me a straight, friendly look from his dark eyes, but did not smile. He was hiding the sadness of his heart behind a stern look that made his face like a piece of rock. Don Sebastián turned from me to my father.

259

"We could go out there," he said. "The two of us could go to Pidal and——" Don Sebastián looked down at his fists. "I think we could get him to tell what he did with Luis."

I could see by my father's face that he was thinking over this idea. Before he thought out his answer, the telephone rang in the study. We all watched the door while Anselmo went to answer it. Anselmo came out at full speed, "Mexico City is calling, Don Agustín!"

Don Sebastián and I stood where we were, watching the study door after it closed behind my father. My mother came to us. "Don Sebastián, won't you sit down and have something to eat? Martín has not had breakfast——"

My mother's words seemed to startle Don Sebastián. He looked around at my mother like a person waking from an unhappy dream. Then he smiled and his whole face changed. His look became warm with pleasure and friendliness. For a moment he looked like Luis. "Thank you very much, *señora!*"

We sat down at the table together. I wondered greatly how Don Sebastián came to be there in our house. I was too shy to ask, and so did not learn until later that his neighbors in the *vecindad* had sent him a message by the "grapevine." This way of sending messages was used long ago, before people learned to read and write. It works like the game called "electricity," in which children clasp hands and send messages. Each child presses the hand of the child next to him. Along the grapevine, one person tells the next.

When Don Bartolo and the other men left our house knowing that Luis had last been seen at Pidal's, they went to the stable where Don Sebastián keeps his burros. A stableboy who happened

to be going downtown gave the message to a bus driver who was going out along the road Don Sebastián had taken. The bus driver told some-one—a rancher, perhaps—who knew that Don Sebastián had turned off on a certain side road. The rancher told someone—his cousin perhaps—who was riding up that way on horseback to see his girl friend. Don Sebastián got the message almost as soon as he would have gotten a tele-gram—if there had been a telegraph line to the village where he was staying. He borrowed a horse, rode to the bus line, and got to Guadalajara just as dawn was breaking.

We were beginning to spoon up the yellow flesh of papaya fruit when my father came and sat down with us.

"Pidal is worse than we imagined," he said.

It would take too long to tell you everything my father heard from Don Gonzalo de la Cruz about Pidal. Besides, there is no use making your blood run cold, as mine ran when I heard the

things Pidal had done in Europe. The main facts were these. Like Don Gonzalo, Pidal was living in France when the enemy came pouring into that country during the Second World War. As you remember, the French army never had a chance because certain people behind the fighting front were secretly helping the enemy, the Nazis of Germany. Pidal was one of these. The Nazis paid him well for this. But that was not the worst. Hitler gave evil men like Pidal great power. They could take away valuable things, like silk and jewels and beautiful paintings, from the French people. Pidal made a great deal of money by taking such things and selling them to the greedy Nazis who did Hitler's dirty work. Also, Pidal spied on people who had once been his friends. When he found a man or woman who was secretly fighting against the enemy, he told the Nazis. Don Gonzalo told my father what the Nazis did to some of these French men and women—things too terrible to remember. Pidal was well paid for his spying. He grew very rich.

263

But the men and women whom Pidal turned over to the Nazis had friends and relations. When the war was over, they remembered Pidal, and he had to run for his life. He arrived in Mexico with hardly a *peso* to his name.

"Pidal seems rich enough now," my father said to Don Sebastián. "But it could scarcely be that such a man would make money honestly. He has been in Mexico too short a time for any honest man to get rich. Let us go to Pidal, Don Sebastián. But let us take my friend the chief of police with us. Though we have no proof that Pidal has done a crime, the police have a right to ask questions of any man with so bad a past as his."

After they left, each minute seemed an hour long. I was so miserable that my mother decided to take my mind off Luis for a little while. She asked Anselmo to take me in the car out to the village of Santa Cruz. As I have already told you, this is Anselmo's home village. It is not so well known as the other towns where pottery is made near Guadalajara. But I was more interested in Santa Cruz because the people there make toys.

I had been wanting to go there for a long time, but I was angry with my mother for wanting me to go just then. I am ashamed to say that I put on quite a scene and swore I would not stir from the house till Luis was found. My mother finally ordered me into the car.

I sulked all the way out to Tlaquepaque—a famous village which has now been almost swallowed up by the growing city. Here we turned off the pavement onto a dirt road. It is a little road that winds among low hills that lie on the Guadalajara plain like swells on the breast of the ocean.

The fields were dotted thickly with young corn of a very tender green. The trees standing here and there in small clumps were plump with leaves. Above us the sky was high and blue and curved like the inside of a huge, deep bowl that had been set down over us. All of a sudden my crossness and worry were gone. Happiness filled my heart like singing. I had not been out of the city for months, you see. I cannot tell you how wonderful it was to get out into the big, free, light-filled countryside with all these green things growing toward the sun out of the red-brown earth.

In one of the fields some men were planting beans between the corn rows. They walked, all five of them, slowly across the field in a line, dropping the beans to the ground and pushing them under with their bare feet. Anselmo stopped the car and called out to them by name. They called back to him, asking how he was and what he was doing out this way. They said that every man in the village was out in the fields except old Marino.

"He's the one we want to see anyway," Anselmo said, starting the car. "The things that come from his hands! If they walked, spoke, and bellowed, one would not be surprised."

The men were wrong, though, about everybody being in the fields. The Flores brothers were digging clay in one of the village clay pits. I had never seen clay dug, so Anselmo stopped the car and I got out.

They were working in a hole about four feet deep and maybe ten feet across. The soil looked

like a layer cake after it has been cut. Above
and below, the layers were brown; between was a
layer the color of chalk dust. Two Flores men
were digging with crowbars at a white layer. They
tumbled lumps of the sticky soil down into the
hole and another brother shoveled it into sacks.

The people around Guadalajara are very in-
dependent and proud. The Flores men worked on
steadily, paying me little attention. It was as if
they were saying, "Maybe you are rich and have
a big car—but still, there are some ways in which
we are better than you."

To tell you the truth, they made me feel very
weak and quite useless. I felt that way until we
got into the house of Anselmo's cousin in the
village.

She was a rather young woman and nice-
looking in the way of a mother. I mean it was not
a young girl's prettiness. Three of her children
were working with her—also her aunt. They sat
on their heels on the floor of their house. It was

a dirt floor, very hard and swept clean. The outside sun was so bright that one was glad the only openings to the room were a door and two small windows. It was shadowy and cool. The women and children had boards in front of them and they were making pigs. One of the girls rolled the clay out thin, and her mother smoothed it over molds that were shaped like pigs. A girl about ten years old put on their ears. When the clay had gotten a little firm the aunt cut each pig down the middle and took it off the mold. Then she put the two halves together, smoothed the edges—and there was a hollow pig of the kind you put money into.

The women and children were quiet at first and looked at me shyly. I felt shy with them, too. But when Anselmo told them about our model, their eyes grew lively. "Oh," the woman said, "you want Don Marino! Go and bring him in, Antonia."

The smallest girl trotted out on her brown feet and in a few minutes we heard the voices of children coming. Half a dozen faces of small children appeared suddenly among the vine leaves growing beside the door. Then there came in a man with gray hair and a gray mustache and a crooked stick which he needed to help him walk, for he was lame.

Everyone said, "*Buenos días* (good day), Don Marino!" most politely. Anselmo got up to shake hands. I could see that Don Marino was very much respected. One of the children pulled a small chair forward for him to sit on. I was sitting on the bench facing him.

Don Marino had eyes much younger than the rest of his body. When he came in, he looked as if he were amused by something that he was thinking. Other looks came and went in his eyes. I thought that he must be seeing the shapes and colors of people and things and thinking how to make them in clay. Somehow I knew right away that Don Marino's thoughts were like mine.

In a very little while he and I were talking together as if no one else were in the room. I told him all about my problems. I explained that when it came to making things like the statue of the saint on the corner of the church of Santa Mónica—and such things as that—I did not do so well.

Don Marino had picked up a lump of clay, and as we talked he gave it a pull here and a push with his thumb there and twiddled it a little with his fingers. Suddenly it was a little goat, looking very much alive and quite naughty. Don Marino gave it some horns and set it down among the pigs.

"Come with me," he said. "We will work a while at my house."

There was grass growing in the street, and big fruit trees hung their limbs far over the walls of the gardens. The town was green and sweet-smelling. Also very quiet—today more quiet than usual, since the men were all away. The only people we saw were women and girls sweeping their doorways or coming and going on small errands. They spoke to us in the clear, singing way that we use in the State of Jalisco. People in different parts of Mexico have each their way of speaking Spanish. I like ours best.

Don Marino lived in a small house with white walls and a tiled roof all covered with tangly vines. He took me around to the back, where he had a tangly garden, and into the house, which was jumbled, though clean. Most of the jumble came from bowls and vases and statues, some finished, some broken, some half-finished, and all beautiful and interesting. Don Marino said he now lived alone.

He showed me things he had made—deer with big spreading horns, and bulls and bullfighters, and *charros* on horseback. Some were painted and some still had their natural clay color. But they all lived, like the stone statues on the church of Santa Mónica. One felt that they could move and were only resting where they stood.

I told Don Marino I admired them very much. He said, "Some thoughts go through the tongue— some through the fingers. Let us see how yours go."

He took a jar of wet clay out onto the porch. I had told him that I could not make Isabela, our fat cook. He knew her, for she had come out to this village with Anselmo. So he set me to work trying to make her all over again. While I worked, he made a woman carrying a jar on her head; he looked up every now and again to watch me. We were sitting on stools, at a board table. Soon he began to give me little hints.

"The neck is longer, even in a fat person," he said, and later, "The skirt must come in a little if you are going to show the foot. Do not get the poor woman off balance."

It was fun—and I modeled much, much better than I ever had before. Don Marino took the little figure from me after a while and held it between his fingers, turning it this way and that to look at it.

"Yes," he said after a while. "The thought comes out through the fingers. If you had been born in this village, you would model very well. One learns these things the way we learn to talk. If you never heard anyone speak, you would not know how words are said and so you could not talk. If you do not see people working with clay, your hands do not know what to do when the thought comes."

He set the figure of Isabela down on the table and twirled his gray mustache. I could tell that pictures which pleased him were going through his mind, for the feeling they gave him showed in his eyes.

"I will come to your house one day each week. Anselmo can come and fetch me in your car. I will teach you what I can—so that your toy city will become beautiful under your hands. It is good to make Guadalajara."

No one had asked him to come—but that was exactly what I wanted. I knew that my father would gladly pay him for coming.

"Good," I said, thinking of the model and what fun it would be to have him show me how to make figures.

Then—as I thought of working on the model—I remembered that Luis would not be there. It would be terribly sad to work alone on the model, wondering all the time what had happened to him. But if Don Marino worked with me I could stop thinking about Luis some of the time.

"Come tomorrow," I said. "Please, Don Marino! Anselmo will come for you early in the morning."

He must have seen in my face how I felt, for he said: *"Muy bien. Adiós, señorito.* (Very well. Good-by, young man.)"

When we got back to the house, I did not see my father's car either in the street or in the garage. It worried me that he had not come home. My mother smiled at me, but she did not look happy. Before I could ask about Luis she said, "I have good news for you. Mr. Johnson is going to stay till the end of the week. I think he and your father are going to start this glass factory. Mr. Johnson will go with us to watch the procession of Our Lady of Zapopan."

I wondered why my mother bothered to tell me such foolish things.

"What about Luis?" I cried. "What happened when they went to Pidal's house?"

"Son," my mother said softly, "do not take it too hard! There is no word about Luis. When they got to Pidal's house, no one was there. Everything was gone except what was in the house when Pidal rented it. The strangest part is that they left so secretly none of the neighbors knew that they had gone."

CHAPTER 21

Dark, Lonesome Road

Luis had stopped breathing when he saw the light flashing on the policeman's badge. It was too late to run. If he tried to dodge, the policeman had only to put out his hand to grab Luis. There was nothing to do but walk on. One step. Two steps. The policeman seemed to be looking straight into Luis's eyes. They were not more than two feet apart—yet Luis had the strange feeling that the man did not see him. His next step put him beside the policeman. Then he was past and letting his breath go in a long sigh. The automobile chugged past, and in the darkness that followed, the policeman's footsteps faded away.

Luis was puzzling about these happenings when he passed beyond the last, scattered houses of a *barrio* where working people live and into the country. The automobile's lights had struck on Luis's own back, but they had glared into the policeman's eyes. The man had been so blinded that he saw Luis only as a blur. But Luis did not think of this. He stopped puzzling and told himself simply that God had not wanted him to be put in jail.

Luis was heading for the *Barranca*. His plan was to go to the bottom and wait until Don Arturo came through on his way to the city from his ranch. Luis had in his pockets only twelve *centavos*. He had no *sarape* to roll up in when he got sleepy—not even a jacket to keep out the chill of night. Yet he felt so sure that he could get along until Don Arturo came that he did not worry.

Luis did not even think that he was doing anything to talk about. Many Mexicans set off on hard, long trips or begin on hard projects with few plans and very little money. They trust themselves to meet each problem as it comes up. And usually they work out their problems. They get where they are going. But often they go a long, roundabout way; and often they get into surprising places along the road.

Most boys would have tired sooner than Luis. This all-night walk was no worse than following the burros with his father, though it was lonelier. He trudged on and on through the night, hurrying as much as he could. Rain clouds pushed up and across the sky. It was quite dark, but Luis could see where he put his feet down.

He saw the glass in time. The sharp, jagged pieces glittered faintly, like a pool of dirty water in the road. In the middle of the glass was a rock, and on this rock bottles had been broken to bits.

As Luis picked his way around the glass, he heard a car. It made a far-off rattling and chugging that came slowly toward him. But when Luis turned around, he could not see the car. He thought his ears must be fooling him, and walked on. But the sound came closer.

Suddenly Luis turned and ran back toward the glass pool. It had come to him that the car must be running without lights. Most of the cars he had come across during travels with his father were old, with tires worn thin. This glass would cut such tires to ribbons of rubber. The driver would not see the glass in time to stop. As he ran, Luis shouted, *"Cuidado!* (Careful!)"

The car stopped just short of the glass. The driver was a young workman who had charge of some of the machinery at the great dam where much of Guadalajara's electricity is made. Most of the time he lived at the dam, eating good meals in a mess hall run by the company and sleeping in the company's bunkhouse. But that evening he had been to town to see his girl and was on his way back in the old car he and some other young workmen owned together. It was what you call a jalopy; the stuffing was coming out of the seats and the lights could not be made to work. He was very thankful to Luis, for he had to get back in time to have a little sleep and go to work early in the morning. If the tires had been cut by the broken glass, it would have been bad for him.

When the young workman asked what he was doing on the road so late at night, Luis quickly decided to tell as much of the truth as was needed. He said that he was going to meet a friend where the old road crosses the *Barranca*.

"You took the wrong turn," the young man said. "The road we are on leads to the big dam."

This upset Luis very much. But the workman said that he would give him a place to sleep at the dam. Luis could make his way down the old road in plenty of time—for it was not likely that a man coming in from a ranch would cross the *Barranca* early in the morning.

When Luis woke, the rocky sides of the *Barranca* still had on their night clothing of black shadow, though the sky was bright. The young workman wanted to show Luis around before time to start work. He was very proud of the dam and the machinery; Luis could tell how much it meant to him that he had a part in making the electricity that flowed on wires from tower to tower till it reached the city. The workman said that several new factories had been started because of this power, and it would mean still more factories in the years to come.

"We do not have very much coal in Mexico," the workman said, "so we can't make electricity with steam engines. But we have plenty of swift streams. The more water we can put to work, the more factories we can have and the more homes will be lit with electric lights."

They went down a well-made road that led onto a great shelf of rock that nature had made on the side of the *Barranca*. From its edge they could look down on the dam. It was wedged into a space so narrow that it seemed like a crack in the rock.

From where Luis and the workman stood, the dam looked like a high, white office building without windows. The river running away from its foot seemed small and still, like a river in a picture of a far-off scene. Behind the dam, a narrow lake stretched crookedly between the *Barranca* walls and disappeared around a bend.

From the lake rose a tall tower of concrete. The young workman told Luis that this was the place where the water began its trip through a tunnel to the machines that made electricity. It was called the intake tower. The water flowed into the tower near its top.

"I'll show you where the water comes out," the workman said.

They went along the shelf of rock for quite a way before the workman led the way to the edge. Looking down, Luis felt an odd excitement, for he could imagine himself sliding down and down till he reached the far-off bottom of the *Barranca*. Four huge, steel pipes sprang from the canyon side and stretched down and down till they reached a building by the river. They rested on concrete foundations steeper than the slides on a school playground. It was such a long

way down that the pipes seemed smaller at the bottom than at the top, though they were really the same size all the way.

"The water goes down through those pipes," the workman said. "Each pipe runs into a steel case about the shape of a watchcase. They are very big. Inside each case is a wheel with many blades set on its face. The water pushes on those blades and turns the wheel very fast. The wheel turns a thing that looks like a huge electric motor, and this makes the electricity. The water goes on out into the river."

Luis had never imagined such a place as the dam with its machinery; his mind could not take it all in. He said, "Uh-huh!"

The workman said it was time to go to work and showed Luis a path which would take him down into the *Barranca*. Luis thanked him very much, shook hands, and started on his way. When he looked back, the workman had disappeared and the great pipes looked bigger than ever.

A workman was climbing up the foundation on which one of the great pipes rested. Iron rods sticking out of the concrete gave him footholds and handholds.

Luis made up his mind to come back to this place when he had finished with Pidal.

CHAPTER 22

Don Arturo and the Hummingbird

If you have never sat under a mango tree, you have missed a very fine thing. Luis sat under one near the old Spanish road where it begins to snake its way up the side of the *Barranca*. Here the road comes curving out of trees. It whipped around Luis like a lasso uncoiling, and plunged into trees above him.

Horses and burros and mules on their way to Guadalajara came into sight suddenly. He could look for a moment into the faces of the men who rode or drove the beasts before they passed out of sight around the curve above.

The sun was high when Luis settled under the mango tree, which had a shape exactly like our cook, Isabela, in her wide skirt. The tree's shadow lay inky black around him, while just beyond, the ground cooked and the grass withered. Above his head the dark-green leaves seemed to talk together as the wind moved through them.

Luis was thankful for those leaves. The bottom of the *Barranca* has much hotter weather than the plain above, where Guadalajara stands. It has a tropical climate.*

The long hours passed; the cool of evening came—but Don Arturo did not. When the moon

---

* If the earth were a man with a belt around his middle, the belt would be the equator. Around the equator they have the hottest weather in the world. You can easily see by looking at the globe that Mexico is not far north of the equator. It is in the part of the world called the tropics. In the low parts of our country, the seashores and the deep, deep valleys and canyons, we have what is called tropical weather. We call these parts *tierras calientes* (hot lands). High up in the mountains we have cool weather, so these parts are called *tierras frías* (cold lands). In between the high country and the low country, we have in-between weather—lovely weather. This kindliest part we call the *tierra templada* (temperate land).

had left the sky over the *Barranca* and blackness shut down, Luis went to the home of some farm people he had met when traveling this way with his father. When he had finished a supper of stew made from river fish, they gave him a *petate* (mat of woven reeds) to spread on the porch. He needed no covers. It was so hot that the whole family slept outside.

Luis was already sitting under his mango tree beside the road when the sun came up. The eldest boy of the family with whom he had stayed brought him some *tortillas* and sat talking with him through the long, bright morning. When they felt hungry or thirsty, they picked ripe mangoes from the tree. They bent forward as they ate, to keep the sticky juice from running down their shirt-fronts. Luis told the boy all about our model, making it seem much better than it was. But he did not say anything about his adventures with Pidal.

The boy went home in the middle of the day and did not come back. His little sister, who came with food for Luis, said that the boy had to help

with the chores so that the family could go into the city the next day. They were going to watch Our Lady of Zapopan come to the church in our *barrio*. When the little girl had gone, Luis felt quite bad for a while. It seemed as if he were going to be waiting there for Don Arturo forever— or anyway, long enough to miss the procession of the Madonna.

He was not allowed to feel sorry for himself very long. A kind of procession was passing by, and Luis could not help but watch it, forgetting his sadness. From below, burros kept coming, some with baskets of golden mangoes, some with avocados, others with small, tropical plums in boxes made of sticks; still others carried bunches of bananas — the small, thin-skinned kinds of lovely flavor that are too tender to be shipped to the United States. All these fruits came from farms at the bottom of the *Barranca,* which is just right for hot-country plants. For hundreds of years Guadalajara has gotten a good part of its fresh fruit from this great crack in the earth.

Goodness knows how long ago the road through the *Barranca* was paved. Moss has grown on the square, well-fitted stones which were placed there sometime during the years when Spain owned Mexico. This road used to be the only way to get to the open country of lonely, open mesas and rough mountains beyond the *Barranca*. It was from this country that Don Arturo would be coming.

Once in the early afternoon Luis stood up as a group of horsemen, with no pack-animals, swept round the turn. The faces under their high peaked hats reminded Luis of hawks. Their lean legs gripped the backs of their small, tough horses as clothespins grip a line. Luis thought of asking if they had seen Don Arturo—for they were surely cowmen from the ranch country. But they looked about them fiercely, as if the city world to which they were going was strange and everyone in it might turn out to be an enemy. Luis decided that it was best to let them pass in silence.

Half the *Barranca* lay in deep shadow when a lone rider, leading a second horse, came swiftly around the turn. He had on a leather jacket and dusty work pants. But his wide hat and his boots were beautiful with designs of gold thread. The horse he led was one of the most graceful animals Luis had ever seen.

Luis sprang into the road, holding up his hand and crying, "Don Arturo! Stop, Don Arturo!"

The rider pulled up his horse and looked down with an impatient frown. "Out of the way, boy! I'm in a hurry."

Luis moved close to the horse's shoulder and looked up into Don Arturo's face. "I've got to talk to you, sir! It's about Señor Pidal!"

At the first words Don Arturo lifted his bridle reins, as if to brush past Luis and ride on. But at the last words he looked more closely into Luis's face. "First you come out of the bushes in Doña Josefa's patio—then you stop me in the bottom of the *Barranca*. Next thing I know you will be crawling out from under my bed. What is it about Pidal? Talk fast, boy!"

"I went to him for a job," Luis said, and poured out his story in a rush.

Burros squeezed by them, scraping their great loads against the bushes beside the road. The drivers muttered angrily. The horse Don Arturo was leading jerked nervously at the rope that held him. But Don Arturo did not move or take his eyes from Luis's face. His eyes grew blacker and blacker until they looked like stormy water seen at night by lightning.

When Luis stopped, Don Arturo looked back at the horse he led and said shortly, "Can you ride bareback?"

"Yes, sir!"

Don Arturo handed Luis the halter by which he had been leading the horse. He said that the horse was named Tzintzún, which is the word for "hummingbird" in the language of the Tarascans. Then Don Arturo watched to see whether Luis knew enough about horses to ride this one into the city. For this horse was well named. His shining bay color was like the wing of a brown butterfly, but he moved in the quick, darting way of hummingbirds—a horse any man would be proud to ride, if he could stay on him.

Luis moved his hands slowly along the rope until he was close to the horse's head. The Hummingbird snorted at him, trying to back off. Luis held him firmly and talked steadily—as you would

talk to a little sister afraid to climb down out of a big, tall tree. The Hummingbird grew quiet. He reached his head out shyly and blew down Luis's neck.

Luis fixed the halter so that it would tighten and gently cut off the horse's breath if he pulled on the rope. I believe the Indians in the United States used hackamores such as Luis made instead of bridles with bits. Then Luis got on a rock, laid himself across the Hummingbird's back, and little by little worked himself around till he could sit up in riding position. The Hummingbird shivered and looked around, as though he would like to buck off this weight on his back. But under the

293

soothing of Luis's hand on his neck he quieted once more.

Luis looked at Don Arturo, who gave him a small smile that made him more happy than many words of praise from a less famous horseman. They started up the steep road together.

As they climbed, the air grew cooler and drier. The snakelike road coiled and uncoiled through tall brush. Even the sound of insects seemed to change, for they were climbing into the *tierra templada*. Looking back, Luis saw the sun touch cliffs of stone rising one behind the other, each one high as a city building. Wind and water had carved them into strange shapes, so they looked like castles and cathedrals and palaces out of a fairy tale. The look of them suited the way Luis felt. To be riding beside Don Arturo on a horse which must surely be the finest in all Jalisco was like his best daydream coming true. Better still was to come—but Don Arturo gave no hint of the idea he was turning over in his mind.

They climbed finally up the last, steep stretch of the old road and came out onto the dirt streets of a little town. The townspeople turned to stare, though they were used to seeing riders of all

294

kinds. Luis knew that they were praising the Hummingbird with their eyes. He sat up straight and proud, pretending that he did not know he was being looked at.

"I haven't told anybody about the Hummingbird," Don Arturo said, as they struck out across the flatland toward the city. "I want to spring him on my friends as a surprise. He'll make people's eyes pop when I ride him tomorrow in the procession of the Madonna, eh, Luis?"

"Yes, sir!" said Luis, enjoying the idea.

"I wonder," Don Arturo went on, "whether you would stay with the Hummingbird tonight?

295

I want somebody who really likes him to take care of him. And I certainly would hate to have him stolen!"

"Anybody who takes him will have to kill me first!" said Luis.

On the edge of the city they stopped to have something to eat at a booth set up in the street. It was almost dark when they reached the center of the city. Don Arturo thought that no one would be looking for Luis on horseback. So Luis got on Don Arturo's horse and led the Hummingbird. Don Arturo went to look for Pidal.

The stable to which Luis took the Hummingbird was the same one where his father kept his animals. It is very near the market in our *barrio*. Luis had been in and out of the place ever since he could remember. He thought he knew everybody there. But a new man took him to the stall Don Arturo had reserved. The other men were busy, and this stable is an odd place that seems to swallow people. Passages lead into courtyards you would never expect; lovely brick archways have been fenced off to make stalls out of long porches. There are little, secret-seeming rooms. This is the reason why Luis happened not to

296

meet any of the men he knew and so did not learn that his own father and my father and Mr. Johnson and many other friends of his were hunting for him. The Hummingbird's stall was a big one, with stone walls and a narrow door. Luis rubbed the Hummingbird down, gave him corn, and waited there for Don Arturo.

He came about ten in the evening. In one hand he carried a sack, and under his other arm, a bundle. The sack was heavy. After Don Arturo dropped it, he had to stand quiet for a moment while he got back his breath. Then he talked swiftly. "Pidal has gone—skipped out. I don't know what happened yet. The chief of police was out at his house this morning and Pidal had already gone, the neighbors tell me.

"When I got back to my own house, who do you suppose was there?" Don Arturo looked at Luis with a small smile in which there was more sadness than amusement. "Don Tomás Topete, the old fool! He was sitting in my library blubbering like a calf and wiping his eyes with his handkerchief."

Don Arturo stopped, as if he were sorting the facts and putting them together in the clearest,

297

shortest way. "About two years ago I gave Don Tomás the money to start a herd of bulls. He's a good man with cattle—but he does not know much about people—especially city people. As soon as he began to make a little money, he began to show off by trying to play the part of a big, rich *ranchero*. He got to playing cards with people who had more money than he had. He lost his own money—and then lost some of mine, trying to win it back. He grew more and more worried—and more wild. One night he bet the whole ranch—bulls and all. He was going to shoot himself if he lost. Of course he did lose, because he was playing with Pidal's man, Manuel, who has great skill in cheating.

"Shooting oneself is a very hard thing to do. Don Tomás went to a restaurant nearby and had a cup of coffee and thought about it. While he was thinking, there came to his table a pleasant gentleman who had been watching Don Tomás play cards. It was Pidal, of course.

"He lent Don Tomás the money to pay me what he owed—enough also to get back the ranch from the man who had won it.

"It seemed, at first, just a nice, friendly thing Pidal was doing. But it wasn't long before he came to Don Tomás with his plan for stealing bulls.

"They stole the first lot—the bulls you saw, Luis—from the State of Querétaro. They kept them on Don Tomás' ranch till they were in fine shape. The hair had grown over the places where the brands had been changed."

Don Arturo gave the sack at his feet a kick. "It was easy to sell them here in Guadalajara," he said. "My friends at the bull ring thought they were doing me a favor—knowing that Don Tomás is my partner! It was as if Pidal had Don Tomás by the throat. The only way Don Tomás could get the money to pay Pidal back was through bull stealing. And if Don Tomás did not pay him, Pidal threatened to come to me and tell how poor Don Tomás had lost my money. Of course Pidal was so clever that no one could prove he had anything to do with stealing bulls. He was clever enough to steal the next herd from Aguascalientes and try to send them clear to the border of California! He would have gotten a hold on your throat too, Luis. Don Tomás was very sad to find you working for Pidal. He likes you."

"I like him, too," said Luis. "Are you going to have him arrested, Don Arturo?"

Don Arturo shook his head impatiently. "I am sending him back to the ranch. I think he has learned that he understands animals better than he understands card games. It isn't as if he had stolen the bulls himself. He just kept them because Pidal made him."

Don Arturo stooped swiftly and dumped from the sack a saddle and bridle that glittered even in the faint light coming into the stall. Luis dropped to his knees to look more closely. He felt the saddle with his hands. He looked up quickly at Don Arturo.

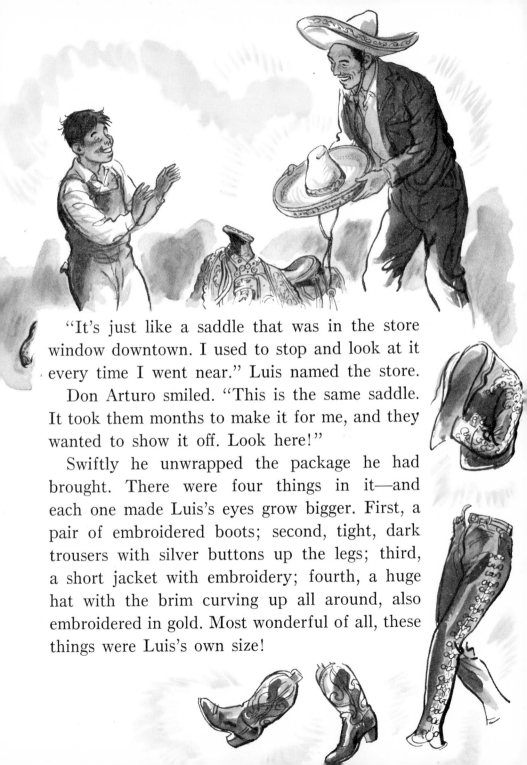

"It's just like a saddle that was in the store window downtown. I used to stop and look at it every time I went near." Luis named the store.

Don Arturo smiled. "This is the same saddle. It took them months to make it for me, and they wanted to show it off. Look here!"

Swiftly he unwrapped the package he had brought. There were four things in it—and each one made Luis's eyes grow bigger. First, a pair of embroidered boots; second, tight, dark trousers with silver buttons up the legs; third, a short jacket with embroidery; fourth, a huge hat with the brim curving up all around, also embroidered in gold. Most wonderful of all, these things were Luis's own size!

"Tomorrow," Don Arturo said, "you will be my stirrup boy and walk beside the Hummingbird when I ride him in the procession of the Madonna. This *charro* outfit was mine. My father gave it to me when I was your age. I've never wanted anyone else to wear it, until now. A boy who would throw Pidal's lie back in his face and speak up for his country is a true Mexican, Luis."

Luis was made very happy by Don Arturo's words, but he was also embarrassed. So he thanked Don Arturo quickly, and said, "What has become of Pidal, do you think?"

"Don Tomás begged me to watch out for him. He thinks that Pidal will try to do something to me before I can make things hot for him in Guadalajara. Don Tomás is very truly frightened. He even thinks that Pidal might try to harm you—because you know too much about him." Don Arturo shrugged his shoulders and smiled. "Myself, I think Pidal is running away as fast as he can. If not, we know what to do about men like him, eh, Luis?"

Don Arturo laughed, patted Luis on the shoulder, and said good night.

Luis lay down to sleep on a pile of fresh hay. It felt like a golden cloud. The munching of the Hummingbird's jaws was music. When one is very happy, all things seem beautiful.

CHAPTER 23

Our Lady of Zapopan–and Pidal

In front of the church where the Madonna has been staying, Luis stands holding the Hummingbird by the bridle. The *chinas poblanas* * have finally come. They are sitting on their fine horses sidewise, their long, spangled skirts fluttering gracefully in the breeze. They are the prettiest girls in town. They sit straight and proud, and now and then send flashing looks back at the *charros,* who are grouped behind

---

* A *china poblana* is a girl dressed in a famous Mexican costume worn only at celebrations and *fiestas.*

304

them. Far ahead, a band is playing. And in front of the girls, Luis hears an odd twanging that comes from mandolins made of armadillo shells. Now and then Luis for a moment catches sight of the bright costume of one of the Indians dancing to this strange music. The Indians will dance all the way to our *barrio*

church and keep on dancing in the courtyard in front of the church.

They have made a vow to dance in the Madonna's procession. This is an important, serious time for them, and for all who will go with Our Lady of Zapopan, and for the thousands crowding the sidewalks and filling the windows all down the street.

Don Arturo is on the church steps, talking to a priest and two important-looking men in dark suits. The others go into the church; Don Arturo comes quickly to get on the Hummingbird, who tries to dance away with him and has to be held tight. Luis looks back, as does everybody else.

Down the church steps comes a little glass house on long poles. It is carried by four men, two in front and two behind. In the glass house is Our Lady of Zapopan.

To understand how we feel about Our Lady you must keep in mind that she is a statue of Mary, the mother of Jesus. In Mexico there are many different statutes of Mary, and we have named them for the towns which are their homes. The most famous is the Madonna of Guadalupe, who is always shown with a sort of seashell design behind her.

When our city was a small town, a great flood almost drowned it out. The waters did not reach Zapopan, so the people thought that if the Madonna of Zapopan came into Guadalajara, the flood might shrink away. When they brought her to Guadalajara, the waters really did go down. This is the reason why Our Lady of Zapopan comes to the city each summer, and why we do her so much honor.

She is made of wood, and is no bigger than a
tiny child. But her power seems very real to
Luis, as he watches her come down the church
steps. She holds herself very straight and
proud, like a queen of long ago. She has a gold
sword by her side. This she wears always.
But she has different clothes for different times.
Today she wears a flowing white robe, with a
large flashing jewel on a gold chain, and a gold
crown on her head.

The men put the Madonna's glass house into
a black automobile. To the front of this car are

fastened two long, heavy ropes of white silk. Each rope is held by twenty-five men who have made a promise to Our Lady that they will pull her through the streets. All together they lean forward, straining at the ropes. The automobile begins to move slowly.

Don Arturo is standing in his stirrups to watch. Seeing Our Lady's car on the move, he touches the Hummingbird lightly with his spurs. The two ranks of *charros* move forward together. The *chinas* are going ahead of them—the whole long procession takes its slow way toward our *barrio* church.

Luis watches Don Arturo and hopes some day that he can manage a horse so well. The Hummingbird does not like to go so slowly. He curves his neck, and his feet make a dancing sound on the pavement. He goes with small, quick, darting motions—just like a hummingbird. If it were not for the firm but gentle way Don Arturo handles the bridle reins and the wise pressure of his knees on the horse's sides, the Hummingbird would dart off, tearing the procession apart.

Don Arturo acts as though he is paying no attention to the horse at all. He does not seem to hear the little murmurs of praise that come from the people lining the street.

Some of the praise is for Luis himself. By the words he catches, he knows that he looks the way he has always dreamed of looking—like a true *charro*. He does not show that he hears, but walks straight and proud at Don Arturo's stirrup.

Behind him he hears no sound except the heavy breathing of the men who pull Our Lady's car. Where she is passing, the crowd grows still and every heart is filled with worship.

Several blocks down the sunny street, the procession stops. The two priests and the men in dark suits carry Our Lady into a long, low building. This is the hospital where the babies of our *barrio* are born. Like all the houses and buildings of our *barrio* on this day, the hospital is decorated with blue and white crepe paper. Little girls in white dresses stand on the steps to meet Our Lady. When she goes inside, there comes the sound of many voices singing. Luis stands still with his hat in his hand. A priest's deep voice comes from an open window. Then there is a silence in the hospital.

Luis knows that Our Lady is being taken through rooms where the new mothers are lying. They would be heartbroken if Our Lady passed the hospital without paying them a visit.

The crowd in the street becomes gay and noisy during this wait. A girl asks the name of Don Arturo's horse; a man wants to know how old he is. Luis does not answer.

From the hospital comes another burst of singing. People kneel on the hospital steps. The crowd grows still. On every face Luis can see, there is a smile as Our Lady is carried to her car. The priests are speckled with bright confetti, and more is thrown as they pass. The people are smiling and throwing confetti because they are so glad—so very, very glad to have Our Lady with them. They feel as though everything will be all right now, for she will watch over them and help them.

This is the way Luis feels. How could anything bad happen to him when he is walking in Our Lady's own procession?

Because of Our Lady, he is not afraid when he comes face to face with Pidal, a block beyond the hospital. Pidal is on the edge of the sidewalk, about twenty feet ahead. He is standing beside Manuel, who has a gun in his hand. It is the same flat gun Luis saw him cleaning in the kitchen of Pidal's house. Manuel holds it close to his leg, where it will not easily be noticed.

Pidal meets Luis's eyes. He touches Manuel's arm, speaking quickly. Manuel glances at Luis, then raises his gun, pointing it at Don Arturo.

It seems to Luis that a voice is whispering in his ear, telling him what to do. He reaches out to take the Hummingbird's bridle, near the bit. The horse stops suddenly when Luis pulls hard on the reins. Scowling, Manuel takes aim again.

Luis points with his free hand and cries, "Don Arturo, look out!"

Don Arturo is used to seeing what to do and doing it in a flash—as one must in bullfighting, or polo, or any such sport. Now he pulls the Hummingbird up till he is almost as straight as a man and his forelegs are pawing the air. He makes him spin round. Then Don Arturo sends him plunging straight at Pidal and Manuel.

They have no time to move out of the way. The horse's head drives between them. His shoulders knock them apart—and knock them down. Once more Don Arturo pulls the Hummingbird up straight and spins him round. No one else gets hurt, though the horse's legs seem to sweep people back. Luis has already come up. He puts his foot on the gun which has fallen from Manuel's hand. But there is no need for this. Manuel is lying still, knocked out. Pidal sits up, but does not try to stand.

A policeman comes quickly through the crowd, shoving people out of his way. Don Arturo bends down to speak with him. The policeman puts one handcuff on Manuel, the other on Pidal.

Don Arturo shoots Luis one look to say, "Good boy!" Then the two of them take their places in the front rank of *charros*.

314

The *chinas* and the other people ahead of them in the procession have not stopped. So quickly has Pidal been stretched flat that they have not known of it. The *charros* let their horses dance forward quickly to catch up. The men strain at the silk ropes, and Our Lady's car moves forward once again.

CHAPTER 24

The Golden Egg

I was told in California that you shoot off fireworks on the Fourth of July and sometimes at large fairs, but not at other times. This seems a sad way to do, for we have fireworks all the year round in Mexico. Hardly a week passes that you cannot hear *cohetes* (rockets that explode in noise but without fire) banging in the air.

We use fireworks to celebrate with a joyful noise the birthdays of saints, of which there are many. The best part of our *fiestas* is the burning of the *castillo*. This word means castle but the *castillos* are in all sorts of shapes, from airplanes to the bulls which are made to leap by the men who carry them. The making of *castillos* is an art in Mexico.

It was thinking of the fireworks to come that kept Luis from growing lonely when he could find neither his family nor me.

He held the Hummingbird while Don Arturo went into our *barrio* church to pray. When he came out of the church, Don Arturo was with the girl who had bought *chiles* from Luis. She was wearing a *china poblana* costume today and looked very happy as she walked between Don Arturo and her father. Don Arturo gave Luis some money and told him to rub down and feed the Hummingbird.

When he had done these things, Luis went to the *vecindad*. There was no one in the place— absolutely no one. All the women and children were in the streets because of the procession, and the men had not yet come home. Don Sebastián was out looking for his son.

"At least," said Luis to himself, "I can have the bathhouse all to myself."

So he took a good bath, put his new *charro*
outfit on again, and went out. He felt quite
grand and still very happy. When he met
grownups he knew, they seemed extra glad to
see him. Luis thought they acted in this way
because of the *charro* outfit, for he still had no
idea that the whole neighborhood had feared for
his life and that many had searched for him.

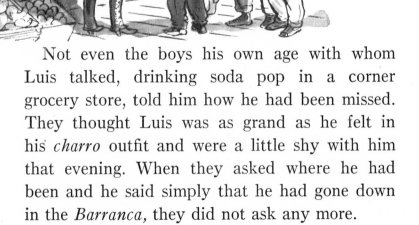

Not even the boys his own age with whom
Luis talked, drinking soda pop in a corner
grocery store, told him how he had been missed.
They thought Luis was as grand as he felt in
his *charro* outfit and were a little shy with him
that evening. When they asked where he had
been and he said simply that he had gone down
in the *Barranca,* they did not ask any more.

It was growing dark when Luis left the boys. Women had already set up little stoves for cooking *tostados* and corn and heating the soup called *menudo*. Their fires of charcoal made a row of glowing dots for three or four blocks along the street. As the dark thickened, Luis walked from one to another, eating as he went. He bought five different kinds of candy from five different peddlers. He bought a balloon for a child because it was crying, and a little windmill for another child because it had such a nice smile.

Feeling very full, Luis came to rest on a corner. All around him rose a friendly buzz of talk, like the hum of the market but more gay. People now filled the whole street and both sidewalks. The excited feeling of a fair made the night tingle.

A dozen men came down the street carrying a huge pole. People scattered right and left out of their way. The pole was all twined around with a framework made of split cane. To this framework were tied things that looked like packages of many sizes and shapes. These were the fireworks; the framework held them in the shape of the *castillo*.

319

It was a very big *castillo*. When the men finally got it stood up, the pole rose higher than the two-story house beside it. On top of the pole was something that looked like a wheel, but Luis could not tell what it might turn out to be. That is one of the best things about *castillos*— you never know what they are going to look like till they go off.

Men with little torches on long poles came and lighted the bottom "packages." At once four fountains of colored fire sprang into the air. They were so hot that they lighted the fireworks above them and pinwheels began to go around like crazy at the corners of the frame. More fireworks lighted above—rockets that burst into colored stars above the rooftops, and Roman candles shooting balls of fire.

Suddenly the whole pole began to turn, for the jets of the fireworks were arranged to push it round and round. Slowly it turned while little bombs exploded to fill the air with all colors and firecrackers crackled like a giant walking on huge peanut shells. The fire ran higher and higher, setting off more pinwheels until Luis grew dizzy as he watched.

320

At last the crackling stopped, and the fire began to creep in silver and blood-red, as if it were climbing a slender vine high in the air. Suddenly the whole top of the *castillo* caught with a burst of gold sparks. It began to turn. It had the shape of a crown all made of glittering, fiery points of light. Faster and faster the crown whirled, while everyone stood silent and staring. When it seemed that it could not possibly go any faster, the crown flew into the air and whirled there like a great wheel of light. It was still whirling when it died, raining bright sparks down toward the dark street.

That was all. As the last spark went out, it seemed as if the fire of excitement in Luis died with it. He felt a little sick from all the sweet and hot things he had eaten. But the feeling in his mind was worse. He felt lost and lonesome and very young. There were dozens of people he knew in the crowd—people who would be glad to talk to him. But the people Luis wanted were those who loved him.

So he wandered lonesomely down the street, looking here and there and not finding anything he wanted to see or do. He was standing at a corner listening to some *mariachis* sing a very sad song when a hand took him by the shoulder so hard it hurt.

The hand turned Luis around and there stood his own father, with Raquel beside him. Tears slid down Don Sebastián's weather-toughened face. He kept his hard hand on Luis's shoulder and held him tight for a moment.

"Hijo! (Son!)" he said, and again, *"Hijo!"*

He kissed Luis Mexican fashion, brushing his cheek most lightly with his lips. But Raquel kissed him Spanish fashion—a good full-lipped smack on each cheek. Luis was surprised to find that he was pleased. Raquel had on a new-looking black dress and a red *rebozo* that set off her good looks. But what made her even prettier than before was the happiness that shone in her face. Everything she said sounded like a snatch of song.

"Let's go home!" She put her arm around Luis and gave him a shake. "Come home, bad boy, and tell us where you have been. I have been dying because I thought you were dead."

The first thing Luis noticed when he got into Raquel's home was a golden egg. It sat

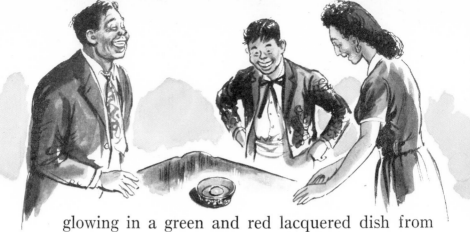

glowing in a green and red lacquered dish from Michoacán, in the middle of a polished table of fine, dark wood. Luis burst out laughing.

His father and Raquel laughed with him. But he did not find out for quite some time how his father happened to bring Raquel the egg. They sat him down and made him tell all he had done from the time he first went to Pidal's house. There were many little cries of sympathy from Raquel, and when he told the part about Manuel hitting him, she jumped up to look at the bruise on his cheek. But Don Sebastián said not one word all the time Luis talked.

Luis knew his father well. The way his hands knotted into fists told his anger more plainly than words. The warm look that came into Don Sebastián's eyes when Luis told how he had spoken up to Pidal made Luis feel better, even, than getting the *charro* outfit.

324

When Don Sebastián told Luis how we had all hunted for him, he was surprised. He was not used to having anyone besides his father think about where he might be or what might be happening to him. Though he knew that he had friends, he had not understood that they cared for him so much.

"I was feeling pretty bad this morning," Don Sebastián said. "I'd been all over the city, chasing this way and that. I got word that people had seen you in every *barrio* and every *colonia*. When I looked these people up, I found out that they had mistaken some other boy for you, of course.

"I was coming along a street in the *barrio* next to ours, when I saw this." Don Sebastián waved his hand toward the shining egg, and Raquel giggled. "I looked through the doorway into a patio and saw a woman making *cascarones*.* She was just sealing up this one with

---

* It is an old custom at dances and parties to break egg-shells, filled with perfume or confetti and colored like Easter eggs, over the heads of the dancers. These *cascarones* are made by pricking two tiny holes in the egg and blowing gently through one to make the yolk and white come out the other. The holes are plugged with wax after the shell has been filled.

wax when I looked. I thought to myself, 'Why not?' and went in and bought it from her and came back here to Raquel's house. I had left Raquel crying when I went out to look for you, Luis. She came very early to the *vecindad* to see if there was news of you. When I saw this egg, I remembered her eyes filled with tears. It would be good, I thought, to make Raquel smile. And I thought that if I talked to Raquel I would not be so discouraged."

"I was bad, though," Raquel said. "I cried when I saw the egg—though I was very happy to get it. It made me remember what a good time we had talking and laughing the night I mended your green sweater." Raquel dabbed at

326

her eyes with a little handkerchief, and went on, "Your father and I felt so sad that we decided to go and watch Our Lady of Zapopan come through the *barrio*. It would be good to pray, we thought, since we could not find you no matter how hard we looked.

"We were standing on the edge of the sidewalk, quite near to Pidal. We knew that Our Lady had heard our prayers when we saw you walking beside Don Arturo, Luis. It was wonderful! Then it looked as if Don Arturo had suddenly gone out of his mind. His horse seemed to be plunging straight at us. Don Sebastián shoved me behind him so that I could not get hurt. I didn't see anything more until the policemen led those two men off to jail."

"I didn't see anything more either," Don Sebastián said. "I didn't even know it was Pidal who had been knocked down, until I stopped by Don Agustín Mendosa's house this evening to see if you were there, Luis. Martín is crazy for joy that you have come back safe."

Don Sebastián explained that it had taken so long to work his way through the crowd that Luis had already ridden off on the Hummingbird when he got to the church. Don Sebastián and Raquel had been hunting for him ever since.

"That's a fine horse!" Don Sebastián said.

While Luis and his father were talking about the Hummingbird, Raquel's mother came home from church. By that time it had grown so late that Luis was hungry again. The women made chocolate, and they were all very gay. It came to Luis that he had the same feeling when he was in Raquel's house that he had in my home. Only it was better—much better, because his own father was here.

At last they said good night and started for the *vecindad*.

"It's hard to leave Raquel's and go home to that place," Luis said.

His father only grunted. But a few steps farther down the dark street he said, "Luis, how would you feel about having a woman like Raquel for a mother?"

"I would like to have Raquel herself for a mother!"

His father gave a grunt that meant he was glad Luis felt this way. "I think—" Don Sebastián said, "I am not sure, but I think that Don Agustín may help me in business. I can care for a wife if he does. The only trouble is, I do not know whether Raquel would marry a rough man like me."

"You are not so rough as you think, *señor*," said Luis. "Myself, I think you are the best father in Guadalajara. Anyhow, Raquel doesn't want a pretty boy for a husband. She would rather have a man, I think!"

Don Sebastián slapped Luis hard on the shoulder. "Hear him!" he said. "No hair on his chin, and he already knows everything about women! But there can be no harm in trying. One day soon I will ask her."

"Why not tonight, *señor?* You are not so slow when it comes to buying a burro you like."

Don Sebastián laughed so loudly that some ducks in the patio behind them began to quack sleepily. He gave Luis a little push to send him on his way alone, and turned back to the house of Raquel.

CHAPTER 25

I Build a New Home

Pidal was sent to prison for only five years.

This made us all angry, because he had a much worse punishment coming to him. The people who were called into the courtroom to tell about Pidal made it clear that he was a "coyote."

In Mexico a coyote is a man who uses sly tricks to make money in ways that cheat the government and the people. Pidal had a clever plan. He had trapped a certain man in much the same way that he had trapped poor Don Tomás Topete. By threats, he was trying to make this man get from the government permission to form a glass company in a way that would make big money. This permission Pidal was going to sell to Mr. Johnson at a high price.

The trouble was that the company would be making its money by cheating Mexico and doing business in ways that were against the law. If this were found out, the glass factory would be

331

taken away from Mr. Johnson. But by that time Pidal would have been paid and there would be no way for Mr. Johnson to get his money back. Even if Pidal were not able to get the false permission for the company, he could not lose. All the money he could talk Mr. Johnson into giving him, he would simply put into his own pocket.

These things, and worse, were told in the courtroom against Pidal. But he was so clever that the only crime that could be proved was the stealing of the bulls. For this, they sent him to prison for five years, and the judge promised to make him leave Mexico the moment he was let out.

As I said, it made us all very mad that Pidal should get off so lightly after he tried to cheat both Mexico and Mr. Johnson, who was a good neighbor. But the punishment of Pidal did one good thing.

Don Arturo Amador began working very hard to get my father elected mayor of Guadalajara. "How," asked Don Arturo over and over, "how are we going to guard ourselves against evil men like Pidal, unless we have our best—our most honest, intelligent men—in the government?"

332

You can imagine that the excitement in our house did not die down even after Luis came back safe. It was printed in the papers that my father would run for mayor. Then our telephone rang night and day; my father went here and there to make speeches and shake hands with people; and there were many meetings in my father's study.

At the same time, Mr. Johnson and my father and Don Arturo were forming the glass company and making plans for the factory. It was a pleasure to have Mr. Johnson come to our house. He was almost always smiling. It made him feel good to be friends with us and to work with Mexicans in the open, "with all the cards on the table" as he said. He had hated the secret plots that Pidal was always talking about. Besides, Mr. Johnson was one of those Americans who really love to build a business. He felt about his glass factory the same way I felt about our model of Guadalajara.

Often he would stand awhile to watch Luis and me or to talk to Don Marino, the old sculptor from Santa Cruz who came to teach me modeling. We were very busy, Luis and I. We could now give all our attention to the model, and we worked many hours each day. With the help of Don Marino's teaching I got so I could make things better and faster.

My father got me an electric train and a lot of track, and we set up more boards on sawhorses so that we could run the railroads and highways out into the country. For the center of the city,

we used Luis's plan of making the buildings by which each section is known. More than this I will not stop to tell you. The pictures of our model show what we made, better than words.

News of the model began to get around, and many people dropped in to see it—not only the friends of my father and mother, but people from Luis's *vecindad* and friends of Raquel. One

day came Anselmo's cousin and all her children, clear from Santa Cruz. And on the day I said the model was finished, Mr. Johnson brought a photographer to take pictures of it.

Don Arturo happened to be in our house at this time. He stood talking with my father and Mr. Johnson while the photographer snapped. Luis was having his picture taken beside the model when I heard Mr. Johnson say, "That boy ought to go back to school. I would like to take Luis back to the United States with me, when I leave the day after tomorrow. But I think it would be better to send him later, if he wants to go. He isn't quite ready to wrestle with school in a foreign language."

My father said he thought Mr. Johnson was right.

"Do you suppose it would be all right with his father if I put some money in the bank for Luis's schooling?" Mr. Johnson asked. "I owe a good deal to that boy."

"I was going to do that myself!" said Don Arturo.

"Luis should have the best education there is," said my father after a minute. "But I don't think we ought to give him his schooling like crumbs from a rich man's table. His own father would be happy to send Luis to school if he were making enough money so that he could afford it. As long as Don Sebastián has nothing but his burros, Luis will have to help him. There won't be time for school—let alone money."

My father stopped and waited to let his idea sink in.

"What did you have in mind?" Mr. Johnson asked.

"Don Sebastián wants to buy eggs in the little towns one can reach only by bad roads. He plans to bring the eggs to the highway on burros, load them on trucks, and haul them to Guadalajara. Don Sebastián has a good head on his shoulders. I think he could make this business pay. I had already decided to put up the money for one truck. With two more trucks, Don Sebastián could haul his eggs clear to Mexico City and make a lot more money. Are you gentlemen interested?"

Don Arturo slapped my father on the shoulder. "I'll pay for a truck."

"I'll buy the other," said Mr. Johnson. "Do you want to form a company, or shall Don Sebastián pay for the trucks out of profits?"

"A company will be best," my father said. "Don Sebastián lacks experience in doing a large business. We can help him with advice as well as money if we form a company."

"It seems to me that you understand what people can do here better than most men," Mr. Johnson said to my father. "Burros and trucks! The new way and the old way! You'll make a fine mayor, Don Agustín!"

It was only a week after this talk that my father decided not to run for mayor. The President of Mexico asked him to take charge of some important work for the national government. It was a great honor—and besides, my father felt that it was his duty to do this work.

We were going to live in Mexico City for a while and then go to the United States. My parents planned to close the house, leaving only Anselmo to take care of it.

The very evening this plan was decided on, my mother threw a *rebozo* over her head and hurried off to Raquel's home. She came back smiling. My mother had asked Raquel to be married before we left so that the wedding party could be given in our house. Raquel was happy to do this and my mother was very pleased— for she loves Raquel, and she loves parties.

It was now the turn of the women to be excited. All the sewing of Raquel's new clothes was done in our house. Raquel's mother came over every day to work on them. She also made dresses for my mother and my sister Lucía to wear to the wedding. There was more measuring and cutting and trying on and fussing than a boy could stand. I teased the ladies so much that my mother finally let me go out to play.

At last the day came. All morning long, neighbors hung around in front of our house, waiting for the wedding party to start for the church. It seemed to take forever to get everyone dressed.

But Raquel looked so pretty when she came out the door that the watching people said "ohs!" and "ahs!" My mother and Lucía looked pretty, too.

When we got back from the church, Isabela and Anselmo, with some helpers who had been hired for the day, had gotten dishes and dishes of food and bowls and bowls of drinks ready. It was a very big party because everyone's friends came—Raquel's friends, who were mostly people who kept small stores or worked in big stores; Don Sebastían's friends, who bought and sold things; Luis's friends from all over. Almost everyone from the *vecindad* was there, except poor Don Bartolo, who was afraid that he could not wash off the smell of his work, and the old *chile*-seller, who said that weddings only made him feel sadder than usual. Mr. Johnson had come back from the United States to get the factory started, and he came to the party with his wife.

My father had hired two orchestras. One played the kind of dance tunes you have in the United States. To this music, people danced American dances. The other musicians were *mariachis,* who played the music for our old-time Mexican dances.

I danced awhile with Lucía and some other young girls, and so did Luis. Then we stood aside to watch. Many of the people danced the old dances very well. But the best of all— the very best part of the party—was when my mother danced with Don Arturo.

The *mariachis* were playing a *jarabe* and my mother kept tapping her little foot where she stood beside my father. Don Arturo came up and made her a dignified bow, though he was smiling under his mustache.

"*Señora*," he said, "I remember that in all the country around your father's *hacienda* there was no girl who danced so well as you."

He offered his arm. My father looked surprised and put up his eyebrows. My mother said, "Oh, no! I am too old, Arturo."

But then my father began to smile and gave my mother a little push. There were others dancing when she stepped out into the middle of the patio, but when they heard her heels begin to click on the tiles they all stood back

to watch. Don Arturo danced the way the Hummingbird moved in the procession, but my mother was like a graceful tree bending this way and that when the breeze blows in the springtime and all things feel young. It seemed as if she could not get tired. One of the men had on a huge hat. Don Arturo took it and threw it down for my mother to dance on. She danced on the wide brim. With her twinkling feet she tied a *rebozo* into a knot when she and Don Arturo were dancing *la bamba*.

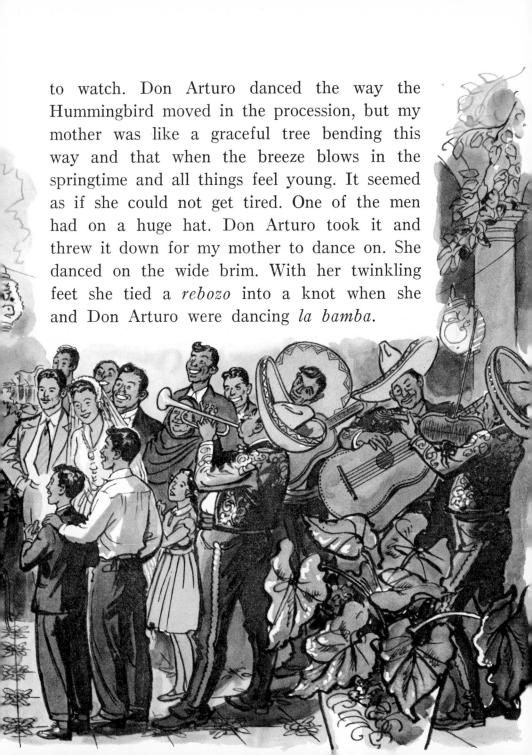

When she was finally done, everyone was more gay than ever. But the good times of grownups make a boy tired after a while. I wandered over to the model and began working on a new part that I had started when the wedding plans were made.

This was the inside of one of the houses down the block from ours, a house that was being made over. Now I was making the last of four small figures to put in this house. My work had grown better since I began studying with Don Marino. The figures looked like the people they were supposed to be.

Luis noticed me working and came over to ask what I was doing. I handed him the figure I had in my hands.

"This is me!" he said in a surprised voice, and turned to pick up the figures already in the house. "Here is Raquel's mother, and my father, and Raquel herself!"

"Yes," I said, "and this is your house, the way it will be when the workmen are finished with it."

Luis put the figures down and looked across the patio. Raquel and Don Sebastián stood talking with Mr. Johnson and his wife; Raquel's fingers were resting lightly in Don Sebastián's hard hand. The two of them looked very happy.

Beside me I heard Luis catch his breath, and when I looked, tears were running out of his shining eyes.

"Martín!" he said. "Now I will have a home, like you!"

Postscript

Amigos mios (My friends):

This is the best way I can think of to let you know what life is like in my city. To understand Luis is to look into the heart of Guadalajara.

> *Adiós,*
> *Su amigo* (your friend),
> MARTÍN

SPANISH AND INDIAN WORDS
USED IN THIS BOOK [1]

Key to Pronunciation

The vowel sounds are the basis for the pronunciation of Spanish, which is almost entirely phonetic. Each vowel in Spanish has only one sound, and the vowels are never slurred as they sometimes are in English. The vowel is held from beginning to end on one tone.

a is pronounced as in *father*

e is pronounced as in *bed*. There are no silent *e*'s in Spanish.

For example, *atole* is pronounced a·**to**·le (three syllables).

i is pronounced as in *police* or like *ee* in *beet*

o is pronounced as in *tone, obey*

u is pronounced as in *rule, rude,* or like *oo* in *cool*

y standing alone is a vowel and is pronounced like Spanish *i*

Combinations of two vowels are generally sounded together. For example, *ia, ie, io, iu* are pronounced *ya, ye, yo, yu,* as in *fiesta* (**fyes**·ta), *palacio* (pa·**la**·cyo). If an accent is placed over the *i,* both vowels are pronounced, as in *María* (Ma·**ri**·a).

ai and *ay* are pronounced like English long *i*

au is pronounced *ow,* as in *how*

---

[1] This section was prepared by Mrs. Margit W. MacRae, Assistant Supervisor of Conversational Spanish, San Diego Public Schools.

ei is pronounced as in *weight*

oi is pronounced as in *oil*

ua, ue, uo, ui are pronounced as if the *u* were a *w*, as in *Guatemala* (Gwa·te·**ma**·la), *cuidado* (kwi·**da**·do). An exception to this rule is that when *ue* or *ui* follows *q* or *g*, the *u* is silent in almost every case.

All consonants except *rr, j,* and initial *r* are much less explosive than English consonants and seem to glide into the vowel that follows. Most consonants are pronounced as in English. Important exceptions follow:

ch is always pronounced like *ch* in *cheese,* not like *ch* in *machine*

c before *i* or *e* is soft, as in *city, cent*

c before *a, o,* or *u* is hard, as in *cat, cot,* and *cut*

g before *i* or *e* is pronounced like English *h*

g before *a, o,* or *u* is hard, as in *gas, go* and *Gus*

gu before *e* or *i* is hard and the *u* is silent, as in *guest, guitar*

h is always silent, as in *hour*

j is pronounced like English *h*

ll is pronounced like English *y*

ñ is pronounced *ny,* as in *canyon*

x is pronounced *ks,* as in English, except in Aztec words, where it is pronounced like English *s,* and in a few words, such as *México, Oaxaca, Texas,* in which the *x* is like English *h* (or like the Spanish *j*)

qu, used only before *e* or *i,* is pronounced like
English *k* (the *u* is silent), as in *picturesque*
z is pronounced like English *s*

No diacritical markings are needed in a Spanish
dictionary, because the letters are pronounced according to the rules above and the syllables are
accented according to the following rule: The syllable next to the last (penultimate) is stressed in
all words ending in a vowel or in *n* or *s;* the last
syllable is stressed in all words ending in a con-
sonant other than *n* or *s.* Deviation from this rule
of accent is shown by an accent mark placed over
the vowel in the stressed syllable, as in *Nicolás, árbol.*

In the glossary that follows, the stressed syllable
is in bold type.

Glossary

adiós (a·**diós**) good-by

amigo (a·**mi**·go) friend

angelito (an·ge·**li**·to) literally, "little angel," used
in speaking of a child that has died

bamba (**bam**·ba) an original dance with quick tempo

barranca (ba·**rran**·ca) canyon with steep, eroded
sides

barrio (**ba**·rrio) ward, district or neighborhood;
usually used in referring to the older section of
a city

calzones (cal·**zo**·nes) old-fashioned white trousers,
tight around the lower legs, often worn by working men

campo (**cam**·po) countryside, open fields

carreta (ca·**rre**·ta) two-wheeled cart

casa (**ca**·sa) house

casada (ca·**sa**·da) married; past participle of verb *casar,* "to marry"

cascarones (cas·ca·**ro**·nes) eggshells filled with confetti or perfume

castillo (cas·**ti**·llo) literally "castle," fireworks on a frame, a set piece

centavo (cen·**ta**·vo) cent

centro (**cen**·tro) center

charro (**cha**·rro) skilled horseman who wears a special costume

chile (**chi**·le) the pepper of the garden

china poblana (**chi**·na po·**bla**·na) girl dressed in the national *fiesta* costume of Mexico

cohetes (co·**he**·tes) rockets, fireworks in general

colonia (co·**lo**·nia) literally "colony," a synonym for *barrio* in the newer sections of the larger towns; a new district or a suburb

conchas (**con**·chas) shells; decorations of silver in the form of shells

corral (co·**rral**) a fenced enclosure for keeping animals; also used in referring to a second patio behind the house

cuidado! (cui·**da**·do!) be careful; take care

fiesta (**fies**·ta) [the first syllable pronounced *fyes*] festival; celebration of a birthday, national holiday, saint's day, or other special occasion

gorditas (gor·**di**·tas) literally "little fat ones," sweet, thick *tortillas* or pancakes

guaraches (gua·**ra**·ches) [sometimes also spelled *huaraches*] sandals

hacienda (ha·**cien**·da) large farm, estate or plantation

hijo (**hi**·jo) son

ixtle (**ix**·tle) a kind of maguey fiber

350

jarabe tapatío (ja·**ra**·be ta·pa·**tí**·o) famous regional dance of Jalisco with a rapid rhythm

jamaica (ja·**mai**·ca) sweet drink made of red flowers

listo (**lis**·to) ready

mamá (ma·**má**) mama

mariachi (ma·**ria**·chi) street musician

masa (**ma**·sa) *tortilla* dough made by grinding softened corn

matador (ma·ta·**dor**) bullfighter whose role is to kill the bull

menudo (me·**nu**·do) a kind of soup made of tripe

novia (**no**·via) sweetheart

olla (**o**·lla) pottery jar or pot

palacio (pa·**la**·cio) literally "palace," seat of government, town hall, courthouse

papá (pa·**pá**) papa

para (**pa**·ra) for

peso (**pe**·so) one hundred *centavos;* used in Mexico as dollar is used in the United States

petate (pe·**ta**·te) thick mat woven of river reeds or palms

piñata (pi·**ña**·ta) pottery jar filled with candy, nuts, etc., and surrounded with a fanciful shape —bird, animal, etc.—made of paper

plumero (plu·**me**·ro) feather duster, or one who makes and sells feather dusters

pobrecita (po·bre·**ci**·ta) poor little one (feminine)

pobrecito (po·bre·**ci**·to) poor little one (masculine)

portales (por·**ta**·les) portico, porches

princesa (prin·**ce**·sa) princess

profesora (pro·fe·**so**·ra) teacher

ranchero (ran·**che**·ro) rancher

rebozo (re·**bo**·zo) long, fringed shawl

refresco (re·**fres**·co) cool, refreshing drink

sala (**sa**·la) parlor

sarape (sa·**ra**·pe) hand-woven woolen blanket

señor (se·**ñor**) sir, or Mr., gentleman

señora (se·**ño**·ra) madam, or Mrs., lady

señorita (se·ño·**ri**·ta) miss, young lady

señorito (se·ño·**ri**·to) young man (seldom used in direct address)

sevillanas (se·vi·**lla**·nas) small, fancy scarves that women wear on their heads

sí (**sí**) yes

tacos (**ta**·cos) *tortillas* with chopped meat wrapped up in them

tamales (ta·**ma**·les) mixture of ground corn and meat wrapped in cornhusks

templo (**tem**·plo) temple or church

tierra templada (**tie**·rra tem·**pla**·da) temperate land

tierras calientes (**tie**·rras ca·**lien**·tes) hot lands

tierras frías (**tie**·rras **frí**·as) cold lands

tortillas (tor·**ti**·llas) flat cakes made of cornmeal

tortillitas (tor·ti·**lli**·tas) little *tortillas*

tostadas (tos·**ta**·das) *tortillas* with cheese rolled up in them

vecindad (ve·cin·**dad**) tenement house

vieja (**vie**·ja) old one, old woman